I0683139

# WAVEMAKER
## THE WAYWARD SAILS TRILOGY
### BOOK ONE

## F.C. SHULTZ

ISBN: 979-8-9930307-1-5

Copyright © 2026 by F.C. Shultz

Daath Stone Books

All rights reserved.

Cover artwork: Gustave Doré; *The Rime of the Ancient Mariner* (#5) and *Orlando Furioso* (#27)

Cover design by F.C. Shultz

No part of this book may be reproduced in any form or by any electronic or mechanical means, including information storage and retrieval systems, without written permission from the author, except for the use of brief quotations in a book review.

*For my sixth grade small group,*
*who are now seniors in high school.*

*Jakin, Kian, Bryson, Cole, Oliver, Justice, Zane, Brett, Jace,*
*Blaine, Rylan, Brian, Zane, Abiah, Thomas, Beau, Noah,*
*Brayden, Tate, Silas, Dawson, Karsen, Brayden , Jordan,*
*Hudson, Gavin, Levi, Link, Carter, Zach*

*Love you guys.*

# CONTENTS

# WAVEMAKER

## F.C. SHULTZ

# I

## THE CALL

The days we'll never forget always start the same as the ones we'll never remember. The rooster crows to welcome the sunrise. The stone streets slowly echo with people on their way to work, worship, or the market. The cool breeze off the sea fills the homes and shops with its crisp saltiness. Two young men in their early twenties shave and trim strips of clean, knot-free cedar into barrel staves and argue about the way of the world.

"It's my Wavemaker-given right to carry it." Searlus stood over a wooden table, sprinkled sand on a stave, and ran the smoothing stone over it. Slowly, the marks of the drawknife faded. It was hot for early spring, and his white linen shirt was soaked through revealing his dark skin. His black hair was short against his head and a short, bushy beard wrapped around his chin.

"Doesn't mean it's smart." Navas gave a last pound to the hot iron band, turned the newborn barrel on its side and rolled it to the corner to join others like it. His black hair brushed against a deep blue jacket pulled tight. His beard was short and patchy. He was fit, like all Horaks who spent time on the sea. But he knew Searlus could pin him in a wrestling match, so he hadn't challenged his friend in years.

"My grandfather carried it on his hip every day of his life." Searlus pulled a blade from its sheath around his waist. "Walked the streets of Tarsa and no one gave him any trouble."

Navas stood and stretched his back. "That was near-fifty years ago, you fool."

"That's my point. We've become like fox pups yipping with our tails between our legs while the Saluman guards ready their muskets."

"And that's my point. Their muskets are always ready. Carrying a sword is just an invitation. Puts a target on you. I'm tired of hearing the crack of a gun echo off the walls of our homes."

"And I'm tired of being treated like filth." Searlus turned from the sanding table to face him. "We belong to the Wavemaker, Navas. Have you forgotten?"

"Do you really want to ask me that, friend? If I've forgotten the beatings? The murders? Is that what you want to ask?"

"I'm...you're right. I'm sorry,"

Navas gave a forgiving nod.

Chatter from the street filled the silence. Searlus shifted his foot in the dust where he stood. Navas continued taking inventory.

"It's just—you heard what they did to Meekah, right?" Searlus said into the silence.

"When you work in the nest you get the claws," Navas said without looking up.

"Something we can agree on, yes. He's still our people. What they do to one Horak they do to us all. The more they think our ways are trite, the less human we become."

Navas laughed.

"We've long been foxes in their eyes, Searlus. It was the same a thousand years ago, even if the hunter had a different name."

"But, a thousand years before that we were the ones loading the muskets."

Navas grinned. "There were no muskets two thousand years ago."

"You know what I mean," Searlus said, apparently not seeing the grin. "These islands were ours and ours alone. King Daw protected our shores. Children walked the streets of Tarsa at night. Women swarmed the white beaches of Kinn."

"And that was the Wavemaker's will?"

Searlus opened his mouth but held his tongue. He knew if he said yes, Navas would point out that in the Letter of Shemwell, the Wavemaker was supposed to be the King of the Horaks, but the people demanded a human king. And if he said no, Navas would be right.

"Horaks of all ages should be able to celebrate the festival without fear that a hot-tempered Saluman guard might be having a bad day and throw you in the stocks for looking at him wrong. That's not freedom. That's not the Wavemaker's will, Navas. We can both agree on that."

"That's the difference between us, Searlus. I don't think about the Saluman Empire when I worship the Wavemaker. They can't help me worship and they can't keep me from worshipping. They're nothing to me."

"They killed your parents."

"You want me to explain the Wavemaker's ways to you, friend?"

"I know the Wavemaker's ways just as well as you," Searlus said. "And I know Captain Finnus from the old stories would not have stood for the abuse we take today. Was he not blessed by the Wavemaker, according to the holy texts?"

"I think it'd be wise if we moved on," Navas said. Searlus was about to interject, but Navas continued. "Rumors are they'll select their crews today."

"Yes," Searlus said.

"That would be something. Sailing up to the edge of the sea, seeing Gildenwood with your own eyes, in all its majesty. Being that close to the Wavemaker."

"Getting away from the Saluman Empire for a few months," Searlus said.

"You're hopeless." Navas laughed again. "I heard your dad might be on the crew this time."

"That's the rumor," Searlus said. "He's been working the docks the past week, cleaning the algae from the hull. Usually means you'll be part of the crew."

"Not a moment too soon," Navas said.

"They've got some bad blood. I don't really know. Dad doesn't really talk about their time in the Lightholm."

"That's too bad," Navas said.

"You know we're eligible, too. Finally." Searlus said.

"You haven't let me forget. We'd be deckhands, though."

"I'd be the High Captain's foot stool if it meant being on one of those ships." Searlus grinned. "I just want to captain a ship one day. And serve the High Captain, of course."

As a boy his father read to him from the holy texts, flooding his mind and imagination from the stories of the old magic and adventures on the high seas. Sailing to Gildenwood is the only thing Searlus ever wanted to do, other than liberate his people. He was ready for the Wavemaker to return to free them from oppression. And, though he had been lying awake at night for the past week, dreaming and agonizing over if he'd make it on the crew, what happened next still caught him by surprise.

The deep bellow of a foghorn filled the Isles of Hor like a sonic flood. Searlus and Navas sprang to attention, stared at each other for a moment, and left the door swinging before the horn ended.

Searlus ran through the main street toward the market. Navas cut off down a side street and disappeared. A young man with a sparse beard ran past Searlus. Older men with long ash-gray beards were walking on the side of the road, in light conversation. Women and children filled the open windows in the stone homes above his head. All faces pointed toward the Lightholm.

The market was absent any Horak men when Searlus arrived. The canopies over the fruit stands cast shadows over the furled brows of the Saluman merchants. He caught the eyes of many disgusted shopkeepers and Saluman citizens.

He didn't care.

He ran past the temple of Sal, where a large stone statue of King Tiveros, the Saluman king, stood in the middle of a pool. No respects were paid in his hurry. Royal guards patrolling the temple pulled their muskets from their shoulders as Searlus took the main road toward the beach. He heard the far-off voice of a guard yell, "Bang!" followed by laughter. He ducked off onto a side street.

"Someday," Searlus muttered under his breath. He cut between the stone homes of Saluman citizens. Clothes hung out on the line between houses, just like his home. Children played with marbles in the street, just like in his neighborhood. The citizens did not look at him with disgust, because they did not look at him at all.

After cutting through winding streets, the stone gave way to hot, white sand. The beach was nearly empty since it was still the first days of spring and the breeze made the water cold. Other young Horak men had already cut their small boats free from the docks and were rowing out into the bay. Searlus did the same. He thumped down the wooden docks, dodging broken planks, until he came to his crown possession.

The wooden, two-seater rowboat bobbed up and down with the calm tide. The wood below the waterline was darker than that above. The name of Searlus' grandmother, Mary Marie, was crudely burned into the side of the small hull that once belonged to his grandfather. A small chain looped through an oar port and on the dock, securing it into place. Searlus pulled a key from his pocket and slid it into the keyhole, freeing the boat from its imprisonment. He began to row.

Once he cleared the docks he let his head swivel while his arms rowed unconsciously. Boats from every island surrounding the Lightholm were floating the same direction. Searlus guessed there were hundreds. And most were filled with three or four men. There were a few lads swimming just off the shore. Navas, and his boat, *The Sun Skipper*, were nowhere to be seen. He did not see his father either.

Three Horak ships, the most advanced ships in all of history, sat in their harbor on the opposite side of the Lightholm. The harbor opened into a small courtyard on the land mass. The courtyard existed only to lead people to the tall tower at its edge, which was growing in size.

The Lightholm was a cylinder tower, but each section told a story with its unique exterior design. Searlus could see the stonework which formed the open archways on the ground level. This was the common area for all Horaks to gather and bring their sacrifices. A few stories up he could see the stain glass histories which framed the Horak library. A cloth like the color of the sunlight through a wave hung down and covered a section near the top. The place where the sacrifices were made. And the crown of the Lightholm, and the Horaks, burning wild and bright, was the flame of the Wavemaker. It burned continually from the time the Horaks entered this land and built the Lightholm many generations ago. The flame was visible from all six of the Isles of Hor.

It was from this section, out upon the balcony, silhouetted by flame, that the High Captain Kaphas emerged.

"People of Hor," he began. His voice filled the bay, though he did not seem to be straining. "My fellow Horaks. The Wavemaker led our forefathers, sails filled with the Sacred Gale, to these great islands, and they became our home."

Searlus continued to row slowly, inching closer. The small boats were packed tight, knocking like wooden wind chimes in the breeze. He slipped in between a boat carrying five young Horaks and a weathered rowboat, like his own, carrying an old man with a short gray beard. The man wore a gold pin forged in sun-shape on his left breast. He worked in the Lightholm. He was a captain.

"The Harbor Stone where you stand is the site of many sacrifices, for the Lightholm has stood hundreds of years as a beacon of hope. The flame of the Wavemaker alit even longer. Evidence that the Wavemaker's promise to our father Hakov still holds true on this day. Because of the loyal love of the Wavemaker, we strive to follow the law which has been graciously given."

When it was clear Searlus could not get any closer, he pulled the oars into his boat. He looked around and saw Navas four or five rows of boats ahead of him. They made eye contact and Navas grinned with satisfaction that he'd beaten his friend.

Searlus shook his head and looked toward the shore. At the foot of the Lightholm he saw men with craned necks filling the courtyard. A wide shouldered man with a dark brown beard stood head and shoulders above the others. Looking closer, Searlus saw the man was standing on a ladder used for maintenance of the Lightholm. The man was his father.

"Because of this faithfulness, we make every effort to remain a faithful remnant, unlike those who have gone to bed with people who share not our blood. We are the remnant of the Holy Wavemaker. We are the sons of Hakov."

In unison, a deep bellied chorus of, "Horah!" echoed in the bay.

"The time has come, as it does every seventh year according to the holy texts, to make the voyage to Gildenwood, where all life began. To bring the sacrifices of the people before the Wavemaker. To be made pure like the rising sun. To make this journey, of which it will be my third, I need a crew. Is my crew among us today?"

"Horah!"

"The Wavemaker has chosen this crew, in all knowledge, past, present, and future, according to his perfect will. As I speak your names, let it be so."

A calm like a wave pool on the shore fell upon the whole bay. Searlus could hear the crackle of the flame high above. Even the hollow thuds of the ships ceased as the water calmed. High Captain Kaphas began.

"Captain Kander of Betzur. Captain Loonas of Shakum. Captain Hemol of Ramooth." An old laugh came from the boat beside him.

"Me?" The man smiled at Searlus and shrugged. "What is the Wavemaker up to?" Searlus didn't reply.

The High Captain continued reading names, and stifled cheers peppered the bay. Searlus knew only a handful of Horaks would be chosen to crew the three ships. Out of the thousands of Horak men living in the six Isles of Hor, it'd be near-impossible to hear his name called. Young Horaks like himself didn't get chosen for the journey to Gildenwood, especially since he hadn't completed his captaincy training yet. Still, he slipped into a daydream of himself standing on the foremast, gripping the cable leading to the flying jib, and looking out over the open ocean as they sailed north.

"Kaius of Ramooth." In the courtyard of the Lightholm, Searlus saw the figure of a long-haired man, with a muscular build, patting a nearly identical man on the shoulder. Searlus shook his head and spit into the sea. The disgust was dissolved almost immediately at the call of the next name.

"Navas of Kedess."

Searlus startled in his boat. He looked across the boats to his friend. They made eye contact and pointed to one another. Then, as if the Wavemaker himself spoke directly, the daydream became reality.

"Searlus of Ramooth."

# 2

## DINNER

"It's only six weeks, right?" a woman with grey streaks of hair pinned behind her ears asked as she brought a small wooden bowl to the table.

"Could be twice that," a bear of a man said from his seat at the far side of the table. He eyed the golden potatoes steaming in the bowl.

"That's how long it usually takes," Searlus said. His seat faced the kitchen and he watched his mother bring another hot dish to the table. "Need any help?"

"Well, yes," his mom said with a smile. "About four hours ago." Searlus missed the grin, and in his silence his mother said again. "I know you were busy. Tell me about it." She put the last plate of grilled tarpon on the table. In unison, they reached their right hands across their bodies and tapped the scar on their neck three times while muttering a prayer.

Searlus took a bite of his fish. "Still eating tarpon?" Searlus said, trying to scrape the pungent fish flesh from his tongue. "You know Yellowfin exists, right?"

"Horaks eat tarpon," his dad said.

"I don't want to talk about fish," his mother said. "Tell me about today."

"Let dad tell it," Searlus picked up his fork and stabbed around his plate.

"You're the man of the hour," his dad said with a mouth full of of fish.

"That's enough, Dovar," his mother said.

"It's not really that big of a deal." Searlus tried to deflect the spotlight. The deflection illuminated something Searlus had not seen since he moved out of the house four years ago.

"Not that big of a deal?" his father asked.

"Enough," his mother said again.

"Holy doman, Elitza! This is a big deal." He turned to his son. "I gave you that gold pendant of the Holy Fleethood when you started your training. I know you know the story of our people. I've taught it to you with my own hand."

"That's not what I meant, Dad," Searlus said, fidgeting with the gold necklace hanging around his neck. His father continued.

"They don't let us keep our own catch. They mock us in our own courtyard. They've seduced some of our people into following their ways. Lote's son works in the King's cathedral, and you couldn't spot him in a group of Saluman filth unless you stripped him bare."

Searlus rubbed the scar on his neck. Every Horak before the age of twelve had three horizontal lines burned into their neck in obedience to the Wavemaker. The men kept it hidden with a collar buttoned up to their neck, and the women wore multicolored shawls. Only in the comfort of their homes, or the Lightholm, did they let it breathe.

"They beat him, Dad. Broke his ribs. Just for fun." His father didn't acknowledge him.

"The journey to Gildenwood is the last part of us that can operate free of the strings of the empire. The beating and the theft are washed away in the open sea. It is the closest to the Wavemaker as most of us will ever be. Almost like he is part of the crew." There was a pause as Dovar's pupils came back into focus and his jaw clenched. "That is what my friends tell me, anyway."

"Always so dramatic," Searlus' mother said. "We have a home. It was much worse when our people were lost at sea for forty years. Were those the golden days of old?"

"They were free," Searlus' father said. He shoved a bite of tarpon into his mouth.

"I'd choose a few foul jokes with a bed to call my own than that kind of freedom every single day," she said. Searlus was nearly finished with his tarpon, bones splayed out on his plate next to half a potato.

"I'll do my best to make you proud," Searlus said.

"And you will," his mother said. "We're very proud of you, son." His father mumbled something under his breath and stabbed his tarpon.

"I was hoping to see Devora before we set sail," Searlus said, trying to steer the conversation.

"You leave tomorrow?" his mother asked.

"In two days," his father said without looking up. His mother ignored the intrusion.

"If she comes in tonight I'll tell her to come to the shop tomorrow."

"She doesn't come home every night?" Searlus asked.

"Your little sister doesn't think 'it's a very big deal' to live according to the holy texts," his father said. "We haven't seen her in weeks."

"She came by just this afternoon," his mother said. "You were at the docks."

"How much did you give her?"

"Excuse me?"

"How much money did she ask for this time?"

"She needed help with laundry, you ox. And I gave it to her."

"I haven't seen her in weeks," Searlus said.

"That was about the last time you came over for dinner, right?" his mom said with a subtle barb.

"Is she okay?" Searlus asked.

"She's making her way," his mother said with a sigh. "I know she'd love to see you before you go. She'll want to congratulate you herself." Searlus only nodded. He remembered a private conversation they shared about how she has been listening to the teachings of a Horak magician. The conversation ended with Devora storming out into the streets of Tarsa under the cover of darkness.

"She's part of a cult, Son," his father said while he cut his potatoes. "We've all but lost her. Can't say it's not nice to see someone fight back against the empire, though."

"Now that's enough," Searlus' mother said.

"Someday the Wavemaker will return," Searlus said. "We'll be able to live in our own land again and keep all our fish and harvest. Maybe this magician will lead a revolt to overthrow the Salumans."

"You talk like that outside of these walls and none of us will be around to see it happen," his mother said.

"You believe it though, don't you?" His mother placed her fork and knife on the table and looked up from her plate. She looked into her son's eyes.

"Of course I do. But our people have been living this way for a long time,. We're making it work."

"It's slavery, Elitza!" Searlus' dad pounded the table with his fists.

"Then take your sword and go," his mother said in the loudest volume yet. His father pushed away from the table, dropping his plate to the floor. It shattered. A moment later the front door slammed shut. Searlus' mother continued her meal in silence.

"I didn't ask to be part of the crew," Searlus said.

"I'm glad you are," she said. "He can get over himself."

"It is a little strange he's never been picked. He's a captain of the Holy Fleethood and works in the Lightholm. It's something about the High Captain, isn't it?"

"Just gossip, Searlus," his mother said. "Best to do the work you've been called to do and be happy you can do it." She backed away from the table and collected the plates. "And, for you, at this time, it's being on the crew that sails to Gildenwood, and I couldn't be prouder."

"Thanks, Mom," Searlus said, looking over to the door.

"You're not sailing yet, though," she said with a grin Searlus couldn't miss. "Help me clean up this mess."

# 3

## THE DAY BEFORE

The sun broke over the mountains on New Casaria, across the Ruby Sea down to the Isles of Hor. A patch of clouds threatened to blow in from the south. Searlus finished sanding the wood for one final order of barrels in the early morning hours. The anticipation of the voyage rose in him like the sun spectacle outside. He was beaming as he smoothed out the planks and fit them into the brackets.

From the open window, he heard a door slam somewhere down the street, and the conversation from the previous night flooded his mind. There was nothing he could have done differently, he told himself. His mom was right about life not being too bad. But his dad was right about the day the Wavemaker would return.

A thousand tiny drummers played on the roof and woke him from his daydream. Outside his window the sky had shifted to a pale grey, and a stream of water splashed down on him from a leak in the roof. Navas

17

thumped down the stairs in step with the rhythm of the rain.

"You haven't fixed that yet?" he asked.

"Have you?" Searlus said.

"Well, as long as we're both asking obvious questions, are you ready to go?" Searlus dropped his mallet and practically skipped to the door. Navas pulled it open and a light drizzle splashed against the stones. Spring days near the coast called for cloaks. Just like on this day, a light rain could blow in from the sea at any moment, and be gone the next, usually multiple times a day. The thin material kept them cool, and the hood kept them somewhat dry. Everyone wore them, Horaks and Salumans alike, because no one liked getting rained on.

"No food, right?" Searlus said in an unnaturally loud voice.

"They'd just confiscate it," Navas said at equal volume. Though the rain was light, the raindrops hit the hood and muffled all sounds around them. They made their way toward the market in the town square.

"Dagger? Cutlass?" Searlus asked.

"Always looking to slice someone," Navas said, laughing and shaking his head. "We're going to be on a ship full of Horaks. No Salumans for weeks."

"We'll have to eat fish."

Navas laughed louder.

"In that case, yes. Please bring a dagger and use it to catch fish. The crew will love you."

Searlus shoved his friend.

"Don't ask me to save you when you get in a fight on board."

"Ah, you got me there," Navas said. "I'm definitely the one who always needs bailed out of a fight."

Searlus shoved his friend again.

"I'll just bring the sword then," Searlus said. "It was strapped to my grandfather's side when he sailed to Gildenwood nearly fifty years ago."

"Don't lose it," Navas said.

"There'd be no point in coming home. Dad would kill me."

"You'd beat yourself up, first."

"True," Searlus said. "Just a new hat then?"

"I'm going to get some leather for my hands."

"Baby hands not tough enough from scribbling in the ledger all day?" Searlus asked in a baby voice.

"These baby hands keep us paid," Navas said. "You should get some, too."

"Pah," Searlus spit. "Basically wearing leather all the time, as rough as these are. Just give me a new cap, and I'll be ready to drop sail."

"You're hopeless," Navas said.

"This is the chance of a lifetime, my friend. I want to look good doing it."

"Hopeless."

The rain let up as they walked, but the sound of the droplet sonata on the smooth stones underfoot was replaced by distant chatter. The market was near, and the local vendors wouldn't turn a profit a single day if they closed shop at the first sniff of rain. Canopies had been extended and hooded figures moved from window to window.

"Meet at Toav's Bakery once you've got your jester cap," Navas said. "I want a cobbler before we go."

"I think the fine lady gloves are that way," Searlus said, pointing the opposite direction. A pair of elderly women passed him with eyebrows raised beneath their shawls. "It was a joke, for my friend." The ladies nodded and kept walking, smiles beaming under their hoods.

To avoid any further embarrassment, Searlus moved from that place as quick as he could. As he walked, he surveyed the shops in case he saw anything else he needed for the voyage. A short man stood behind a table full of fresh oranges and mangos. His stand was the busiest as people gathered supplies for their meals that day.

Next to him was an identical table, with food laid out in an identical way. Rows and rows of fresh fish lined the table. The sun was shining now, reflecting off the massive blue scales of the tarpon. Four fish were laid flat, covering the length of the table. The man behind the table noticed the rain had stopped for this moment and pulled back his hood. He was not wearing a shirt under his cloak, likely because he had been out fishing just that morning and it had been soiled at sea. Searlus saw the three-lined scar on the man's neck. The man locked eyes with Searlus, shuddered, and pulled his cloak up to cover it. Searlus put up both hands, palms out, to comfort the man, before pulling down his hood and revealing his own scar. The man nodded and returned to his fish, keeping his cloak covered.

*Dad is right*, Searlus thought.

Searlus waded through the crowd as his mind wandered back to the previous night's conversation yet again. Only this time, he was interrupted by a lady carrying a large woven basket full of clothes. She turned the corner and crashed right into him. The basket splashed to the wet ground.

"Sorry, sorry, sir," the woman said with her eyes diverted. She knelt and tossed the clothes back into the basket.

"You really should slow—Dev?" Searlus said. The woman looked up and a wave of relief washed over her face.

"Searlus!" she said as she stood and wrapped her arms around her brother.

"Missed you last night," he said as she let go of him.

"I've missed you this past month," she said.

"Been busy at the shop."

"What do you think I've been doing?" She motioned to the clothes still scattered in the road.

"I heard rumors you've been helping the Salumans."

"Whose laundry do you think this is?"

"Not just with laundry, Devora. What were you really doing last night?"

"Stop it, Searlus," she said with a quiver in her voice. "I'm making it. Trying to do it honest with all this, but if they give me a chance to make a little extra, I'm going to take it," Devora said. "They don't give me much trouble. Now help me clean this up." They knelt and refilled the basket with the damp clothes.

"Fine, but I'm worried about you," Searlus said. His sister didn't say a word, so he moved on. "Speaking of trouble, you missed quite the spectacle last night."

"Dad lose it again?"

"Again?" Searlus asked.

"Got into a little tussle with some Saluman teens not much older than you. Nothing really. Told us about it that night. Mom told him to let it go. He didn't like that. Stormed out, breaking the door off the hinges when he slammed it."

"Salumans," Searlus said under his breath.

"You mean, teenagers," Devora said as she stuffed the last linen in the basket and picked it up. She propped it against her hip to help bear the weight. "What happened this time?"

"He didn't make the crew for the voyage to Gildenwood."

Devora laughed.

"Hardly something to get that angry about. Almost no one gets chosen."

"I did," Searlus said.

"What?" Devora said, smiling big again. She dropped the basket and the clothes spilled out again. "Yay! Good for you. When do you leave?"

"First thing in the morning."

"I'll let you get back to packing then. I've got to get these washed, anyway," she said as she knelt to load up the basket. "Glad I ran into you."

"One more thing," Searlus said. "The magician?"

"That's what you're most concerned about?" Devora asked. "I just told you I'm barely scraping by, spending my nights with Saluman guards, and you're worried about me listening to the teachings of a Horak?"

"I just want you to be safe," Searlus said.

"Since when is safety the point? You wouldn't be leaving tomorrow if it was."

"That's different," Searlus said. "It's what the Wavemaker commands."

"Seems the same to me," Devora said. "Besides, I haven't listened to him teach in a long time. Been a little busy."

"Good."

"He'll be in Kedess for a meal to end the Festival of Floats tomorrow night. I'm going. Don't say a word about it to mom and dad."

"Dev—"

"I've got to go," she said, picking up the basket again. "Tell mom and dad I'm doing fine and I'll stop by soon." Before Searlus could reply, she tossed her cloak up over her head, adjusted her grip on the basket, and disappeared into the crowd of people. The desire to follow his sister to tell her he just wanted her to be safe was in conflict with his desire to preserve his rugged appearance. He wanted to be a foundation for the family, especially as their father was starting to lose it. By the time these thoughts had flashed across his mind, Devora was gone. He couldn't have caught up to her if he wanted to.

He walked in a near trance, half looking for a vendor that sold clothes, half lost in his thoughts. Unhooded heads bobbed up and down, filling the marketplace. Most of the men wore a wool cap. Women had their hair tied up in shawls. The Saluman guards on patrol wore tricorne hats. The only head void of any covering was

Searlus'. He eyed a shop with headwear displayed on a table and got in line.

Searlus had heard it gets unbearably cold the farther they sail to the north. All he wanted was a tight knit cap he could wear day in and day out on the ship. He surveyed the table as the man in front of him shopped. A row of simple gray caps, that would fit snug around his head, caught his eye. It must have been a great hat, because the man in front of him bought one, too.

"I'll take one of those gray ones," the man said.

"Ah, yes. Very good hat," the middle-aged shopkeeper said. "My wife makes them very strong. Nine copper."

"Last one fell into a well," the man in front of him confessed. He counted out a few coins and handed them to the vendor.

"Soak it in the coldest water you can find. That'll keep it nice and snug," the vendor said.

"Thank you, kindly."

The man took the hat, nodded to the vendor, and went on his way. Searlus approached the table with a large smile, as if the fact that two of the same hats being purchased back-to-back was a hilarious cosmic coincidence. The vendor took one look at Searlus' dopey grin and furled his brows.

"What do you want?"

"Funny enough, I'll take one of those gray caps, too."

"Thirty copper." The grin on Searlus' face disappeared. The joke was up. Searlus could feel his cheeks getting warm. He pushed his lips together until he gathered his thoughts.

"Sorry, sir," he said. "I might have been unclear. I'll

take just one of those gray caps, just like that man before me."

"Thirty copper," the man said.

"You just sold it for nine," Searlus said.

"Now it's thirty."

"I don't have thirty copper."

"Then get lost."

The heat spread down to Searlus' neck and into his chest. He pulled the front of his cloak to cool down, and that's when he realized his scar was exposed. This wasn't a case of a vendor playing a cruel joke, it was because Searlus was a Horak.

"You can't do that," Searlus said.

"Leave," the vendor's voice grew louder.

"I'm not leaving without a hat," Searlus matched his volume. The people in line behind Searlus started murmuring. The next moment they had dispersed. And a moment after that, before Searlus could react, two Saluman guards had approached the table, surveyed the scene, and spotted Searlus' scar.

"This kid causing you trouble?" one of the guards said to the vendor.

"Doesn't like my prices," the vendor said.

"He's charging three times what it's worth," Searlus said.

"Shut up," the guard said. The heat had spread down to Searlus' toes. He understood what would cause his father to slam a door off its hinges. That burning anger flowed through him now. The guard and the vendor had been talking, but Searlus only now picked up on their conversation.

"Yes, he needs to go," the vendor was saying.

"I just want to buy this hat," Searlus said. The Saluman guard slapped Searlus' across the cheek, knocking him to the ground.

"I told you to shut up, mutt."

The two guards grabbed Searlus by the arms and drug him away from the vendor's table. The vendor cracked a satisfied grin as Searlus was hauled off. The guards drug their culprit across the market and threw him against the wall.

"Trying to steal from the Saluman Empire, were you?" the guard who had slapped him asked.

"No," Searlus said. Both guards pulled short wooden clubs from their waists.

"Don't lie, boy," the second guard said. The words were punctuated with a thud of the club to human flesh. One after the other.

"Searlus!" a familiar voice called from behind the beating. The Saluman guards stopped their barrage. Navas ran up to the scene.

"You know this fussock?" the second guard asked.

"Yes, sir," Navas said. "My brother. We don't let him wander the market alone. I've been looking all over for him. I apologize if he's caused any trouble."

"Trying to steal from King Tiveros," the first guard said.

"Oh, it can't be!" Navas said. He slapped Searlus across the cheek. This satisfied the guards and they holstered their clubs.

"Keep him on his leash," the second guard said.

"Yes, sir. Of course, sir," Navas said. The guards gave

Searlus one last look before turning and returning to the square. Navas waited until they were out of earshot before he helped his friend up from the dust. "What is wrong with you?"

"Me?" Searlus said. "They can't just go around beating anyone they choose."

"What did you do?"

"Nothing!" Searlus said. "I am a Saluman citizen just like them. Born in a Saluman province. I'm going straight to the governor's office." Navas grabbed the sleeve of Searlus' cloak.

"Then what?" Navas asked. "They'll throw you in jail until the hearing, and who do you think they'll side with? I don't even know what you did, but I know no one is going to believe a dirty, dark-haired Horak."

"They need to be punished," Searlus said, looking off in the direction where the guards had disappeared.

"You'd rather have two low-down Saluman guards to be tried and punished than to set sail for Gildenwood in the morning?"

Silence filled the space between them as Navas' words sunk in. In the scuffle, Searlus had forgotten the reason he came to the market in the first place; to buy a hat for the voyage. He was leaving this place, if only for a few months. The trip couldn't come soon enough.

"Fine," Searlus said.

"That's what I thought," Navas said. "Now, let's go get that pie and start packing. We've got to be at the Lightholm before sunrise."

# 4

## SETTING SAIL

Searlus and Navas beat the sun to the docks the next morning. The sea came in slowly and caused the small boats to knock together. In the distance, Searlus could see the dark shadows of three ships in port around the Lightholm. The path down the docks was lit by torchlight. Searlus planned to pack everything up in his little rowboat, but a small passenger boat bobbed up and down in the dancing flames.

"You boys going to the Lightholm?" a voice called out from the boat. A man rose from the shadows within the vessel as Searlus and Navas approached.

"Yes, sir," Navas said.

"Name," the man asked.

"Navas of Kedess."

"And you?"

"Searlus of Ramooth."

The man let out a single laugh.

"Dovar's boy?"

"Yes sir," Searlus said. The old man pulled a piece of

parchment from inside his cloak and ran his fingers down it, stopping twice. A moment later he rolled it back up and tucked it away.

"Come on, then," the man said. Searlus and Navas grabbed their bags and made their way to the boat. Searlus gave his rowboat a little nod as he walked past. They stepped down into the boat and found four other Horaks spread out on the four benches inside. "Grab an oar," the voice came from the front of the boat. No one said a word. They each found the long piece of wood at their feet and began rowing in unison. The old man was at the helm, guiding them to the small island ahead.

As their makeshift crew stepped off the ferry and into the courtyard of the Lightholm, the first light of morning had begun to fill the sky. The three ships which Searlus had only seen in shadow from the docks of Tarsa were now larger than life in port on the opposite side of the courtyard. The three ships floated in a line, each with three tall masts that rose into the sky, challenging the Lightholm's height. The dark brown wooden hulls bobbed up in down in the water. Portholes rounded with gold dotted the side of the ships. A complex cobweb of ropes and pulleys crisscrossed from foremast to main mast to mizenmast. Despite never sailing aboard these ships, Searlus knew them well. All Horaks did. They were the pride of the Royal Fleethood. The two ships in the rear were called *Noak Tava* and *Gomoshah*. Then, at the front of the procession, was the crown jewel. The largest, most advanced, ship ever constructed.

*Gildenglory*.

The two less impressive ships had retained their

original names in the old Horak tongue. The *Gildenglory* had been called many names in her storied history. In recent years, the last four or five hundred, High Captains had taken it upon themselves to christen the vessel with a name of their choosing. This is usually done as the culmination of the ceremony to celebrate their promotion to the High Captaincy. Searlus had never known her by any other name.

"Shove off," an old man said bumping into him.

Searlus was pulled from the splendor of the massive ship by the flurry of activity in the courtyard. Men of all ages moved in and out of the Lightholm like ants to an anthill. They crisscrossed over the dark black, perfectly circular Harbor Stone in the middle of the courtyard, carrying boxes of food and barrels of fish. Four men passed them carrying a wooden chest with a lock secured to the front.

"Name," a different, high-pitched voice called out behind them. They whipped around and saw the gold sun emblem pinned to the man's shoulder. He was a tall, thin fellow, and the only Horak man Searlus knew who didn't have a beard. Something about his voice stirred up an unjustified annoyance in Searlus. But they all complied and Captain Nimrad began barking orders to them.

"Searlus of Ramooth," the captain said, looking up. Searlus raised a hand. "All the barrels from the kitchen need loaded."

"Alright," Searlus said, making his way to the Lightholm.

"Excuse me?" Captain Nimrad asked.

"I mean, yes, sir," Searlus said. Captain Nimrad nodded his hairless face and continued giving orders to the other Horaks. Searlus looked at Navas and shrugged his shoulders. Navas shook his head and smiled. They parted ways and got to work.

Searlus slung his bag over his shoulder and made his way to the stone archways at the edge of the courtyard. The dark gray arches wrapped around the whole bottom floor of the Lightholm, making it possible to see straight through and out the other side. The sun was rising now and the whole ground floor was illuminated with the morning glory. A Horak flag flew suspended above every archway, and Searlus passed under one as he entered the Lightholm.

The floor was a patchwork of ornate blue tiles all pieced together. The rotunda ceiling was open four stories high, with the third story opening to a balcony overlooking the courtyard. The walls were painted with the words from the holy texts, and repeated in their entirety over and over, round and round, all the way up. Four stairwells wound around the wall of the rounded Lightholm, each equidistant from each other, and all were full of men carrying supplies down. Searlus made his way up the stone staircase closest to him.

He made it to the floor just above the rotunda. Tables and chairs filled the room. Searlus had eaten here many times during his training to be a captain. The first time he came to the Lightholm he was only four years old and sat in this very room for the Feast of High Tides with his father. He loved the way the men sang the sea shanties of old, and how some of them got to live in this holy place.

Searlus had been studying ever since. Years and years of study and memorizing the holy texts, of learning the ways of the Lightholm. He was on pace to be an official captain within the year.

The wide, golden stairway shone on the far side of the banquet room. It split and wound around the side of the Lightholm and disappeared out of view. Searlus knew that was where the real work was done. Only the captains could enter the higher levels of the Lightholm, and only the High Captain himself could enter the throne room of the Wavemaker. Searlus had heard stories, rumors, and tall tales about what took place up there. He dreamed of being able to ascend those golden stairs someday.

"Get to work," a voice called from the corner of the room. A barrel-shaped man yelled at Searlus and pointed to stacks of food supplies stacked against the wall. Searlus obeyed and grabbed a barrel and carried it down to the shipyard.

...

Searlus spent the whole morning going up and down the Lightholm stairs, carrying barrel after barrel. Men of all ages were going up and down the stairs, carrying crates and barrels. With every trip to the courtyard, more and more people filled the common area and the Harbor Stone. Horak people were sailing their little boats over from the surrounding islands. On another trip down from the kitchen, Searlus noticed a handful of Saluman guards now mixed in with the Horaks. They fanned out around the perimeter of the small island and each had a long musket slung over their shoulder.

Around noon Searlus made his way back to the kitchen to find a single barrel against the wall. He entered the room the same time as a teenage Horak.

"I'll get it," Searlus said, looking to kid.

"I'll get it, old man," the kid said. Searlus laughed.

"I get it. Got to prove yourself," Searlus said. "What's your name, kid?"

"Jok," he said. He walked over to the last barrel and gave it a bear hug before lifting it off the ground. "And I'm not a kid. I'm fifteen."

"You're right, Jok. They don't let kids on these ships. You on the *Gildenglory*?"

"Wouldn't that be something," Jok huffed as he walked past Searlus with the barrel in his arms. He made his way to the stairs.

"Can you even see where you're going?" Searlus called out.

"I've got it, grandpa," Jok called back. His voice echoed off the stone walls as he disappeared down the steps.

Searlus did one more sweep of the large room before making his way down the stairs. This time, before he made it to the ground floor, the murmur of the crowd outside filled the Lightholm. They knew it was almost time for the ships to depart. Searlus knew it, too.

He wove his way through the crowd, watching where he was going, but also looking for a few familiar faces. He succeeded only in that he did not run into anyone on his way to the main ship. As he approached the ramp up to the ship, he saw a man with a weatherworn tricorne hat standing in a group nearby. Anger welled up in Searlus. Saluman guards shouldn't be on the same soil as the Lightholm. The crowd fell silent.

Searlus was nearly to the ramp, about to board the ship, when a Saluman officer, not dressed in the solider attire, but wearing a deep red overcoat with a white undershirt, and a crisp tricorn hat stepped onto the ramp. Searlus wasn't sure if the crowd had been silenced by this attempted desecration, or by the figure descending the ramp.

High Captain Kaphas walked down toward the Saluman officer.

The High Captain wore a wide-brimmed hat, with a gold band around the base. His skin was pale and a long beard hung from his chin. A sky-blue outer coat hung down to his knees with dark brown leather pants beneath. Six gold necklaces hung from his neck, each at varying lengths, signifying the six Isles of Hor. Beneath the gold chains and the outer coat was white linen that had been dyed with swirling reds, yellows, and oranges. His hands were bedecked with gold rings adorned with ruby and sapphire stones. Inside the outer coat, Searlus spotted a small pistol strapped to his hip.

"High Captain Kaphas," the Saluman officer said for the whole Lightholm to hear. By this time, Searlus was at the bottom of the ramp, but forced to stay put by the remaining Saluman guards. "By decree of King Tiveros, with the intention of learning the ways of the high seas and expanding trade routes, Saluman Elite Officer Vorenos, speaking, will be accompanying you on your voyage, which has been approved by the seal of Sal."

A collective gasp rolled over the crowd. Searlus wanted to scream in opposition. That wasn't how it's supposed to be. Only Horaks can travel to Gildenwood. This was the only freedom they had left. The whole island cast their eyes upon the High Captain. His face was solid stone and his eyes burned under the shadow of his hat. He shifted his eyes from the Saluman officer standing midway up the ramp, and addressed the crowd gathered before him.

"Captains of the Holy Fleethood. Horaks from all islands of our great land. Today is a great day. For today these three ships, loaded with your sacrifices, set sail toward the good land of Gildenwood to offer a penance for our lawlessness, which the good Wavemaker so graciously allows. Do pray the Sacred Gale fill our sails, and the Wavemaker be at the helm."

With that, the crowd cheered, and the High Captain stepped aside and nodded to the Saluman officer. The officer returned the nod and made his way onto the ship. Searlus followed behind with his barrel, passing by the High Captain. No eye contact was made. The High Captain was busy waving to the crowd.

After Searlus loaded the barrel in storage, he returned to the deck to find all the Horak crew members waving over the side of the ship. The ramp had been pulled on-board, but baskets still hung over the side of the ship every few feet. Horaks in the courtyard made their way to the ship and tossed in last second sacrifices, by way of gold coins, into the baskets.

Searlus scanned the crowd but had trouble identifying any faces in the scramble.

"Stand by to make sail!" a familiar high-pitched voice yelled behind him. Captain Nimrad stood addressing the crew. The High Captain was nowhere to be seen. Searlus looked over the side one more moment and found what he was looking for. He locked eyes with his mom and waved. Beside her was his sister, smiling and waving, but Searlus didn't smile back. Immediately he noticed his sister's eye was swollen black and blue. Worry washed over his face. Captain Nimrad yelled again, "It's not too late to throw you overboard." Searlus was pulled away from the side of the ship and spun around to face Captain Nimrad. "Get to work, you bilge rat," he said.

"Yes sir," Searlus said. He scurried across the deck and began uncoiling the ropes which led to the foresail in the front of the ship. In the mix of worry for his sister, and panic for his responsibilities on the crew, it hadn't registered that someone was missing from the courtyard.

His father.

Anger fueled his work to get the ship ready to sail. Shortly after Captain Nimrad called for the sails to be dropped, they were leaving the harbor. Searlus leaned against the foremast to rest and think, but before he touched the wood, that familiar whine cried out.

"Attention, Horaks. High Captain on deck!"

# 5

## A SALTY WELCOME

The *Gomoshah* and the *Noak Tava* sailed parallel to the *Gildenglory*. Searlus and Navas stood at attention near the foremast as the High Captain came out of his quarters onto the main deck. He still wore the full wardrobe of the Royal Fleethood. All the Horak sailors stood in silence as he made his way up a flight of stairs toward the quarterdeck. The light breeze carried them gently through the bay and the Lightholm shrank in the distance, along with the southern islands.

"May the Wavemaker's will be done this day, and those that follow," the High Captain said from the raised quarterdeck. His voice filled the main deck, only rivaled by the splash of the ships gliding across the sea. "Our forefathers have been making this trip since Hasha returned home with our people after sailing these seas for forty years. It is what the Wavemaker wills. Thus, it is our will."

The door of the High Captain's cabin opened and the Saluman Elite Officer Vorenos appeared in the doorway. All eyes shifted to the outsider. The Saluman officer joined the crew on the deck and looked up toward the High Captain. His bright red jacket stood out like a fire at sea amidst the Horak crew's cloaks of green and grey earth-tones. A gold pendant on his chest bore the insignia of the Saluman Empire. The sun reflected off the eagle with wings outstretched over water, mountains, and clouds.

"This is not a safe voyage," the High Captain continued. All eyes shifted back to him. "But it is right. We all must do our part to keep the ship clean. If sickness or disease find their way in our quarters, you will wish you'd never set foot on these decks.

"We know calm seas around the Isles of Hor, praise be to the Wavemaker, but ahead lies the Sea of Beasts, where the storms are frequent as the breeze and the Coiled Whale dwells. For the sake of your fellow Horak, say your prayers before each watch."

Searlus and Navas looked at each other. They'd heard the stories of the seas beyond their islands, but there was always a hint of the fantastic in the telling. This was different. The High Captain spoke with authority and conviction. The kind of authority and conviction that comes from seeing something first-hand.

"There will be death. No voyage to Gildenwood has been made without loss. But, though the Wavemaker's will remains a mystery to us lowly seafarers, to die serving the Wavemaker is the greatest honor. You will be forever remembered among our ranks. But death is not the peak of our concerns." The crew shifted in a collective unease.

Whispers filled the deck before the High Captain continued.

"No, there is a threat more vile than disease, more wicked than the Coiled Whale, and more unsettling than the storms." He let a silence hang over the deck. He surveyed the two smaller ships. They're crews were silent. "Zamarians," he said nearly spitting.

"The Zamarian bastards will do anything to seize our ship to satisfy their debauchery. They fly a desecrated Horak flag. Solid black with a single white dot in the middle. We are the only people who know how to sail the high seas. If you see a ship on the horizon, report it to the first mate immediately. The Zamarian filth will not interfere with our voyage again." The High Captain paused and regained his composure. When he spoke again the anger in his voice had faded.

"As we near Gildenwood the Wavemaker will provide a luneshark for the sacrifice. They are the most beautiful creature in the sea, rivaled only by Gildenwood itself where the trees are solid gold, from the trunk to the leaves. In the distance it looks like another sun setting on the horizon. You are in for a treat, my friends. I wish I could see it again for the first time. It is like nothing else in this world, for it belongs to another."

He let the silence hang for a moment, so the imaginations of the crew could wander. Then, he nodded to a man much older than himself, possibly the oldest man in the crew, and the man hobbled up the stairs and joined him on the bridge.

"We have a great wayfinder with us on our voyage. Wayfinder Meeha will help us cut a path to Gildenwood.

If we all do our part, the Wavemaker will be with us, and the Sacred Gale will fill our sails. Who could be against us? Listen to your first mate and keep an honest watch. I'll see you all at dinner to celebrate the end of the festival. They're all yours, Captain Nimrad."

Applause broke out on the deck of the *Gildenglory*. The other two ships quickly followed. The High Captain waved to each ship and took a half bow before leaving the quarterdeck and making his way back to his quarters.

"You heard the High Captain," Captain Nimrad shouted in his squeaky voice. "Drop the main sails. Pull the offering baskets onboard. Get the rest of these barrels below deck. Man topgallant halyards and sheets. Lay aloft and loose fore topsail! Out mizzen course! Move it, you petulant rapscallions!"

# 6

## THE FIRST NIGHT

Searlus was used to the manual labor required for a hard day's work. Making and transporting barrels all day required strong hands and dedication. He figured he'd have no trouble with the tasks required of the crew, especially compared to most of the other captains who lived in the Lightholm and read from the holy texts all day.

The only time he was more wrong is when he was a kid and thought his sister would want a pet jellyfish in her bed.

By the time night fell, and the three ships were tethered together, the muscles in Searlus' back were sore. He struggled to sit back against a chair. He stayed seated while most of the other Horaks from all three ships sang and danced at dinner that night. His back wasn't the only thing bothering him, though. He winced as he reached across his body and tapped the scar on his neck three times before picking up some fresh tarpon with his rope-burned hands.

"Want me to feed it to you?" Navas said with a mouthful of food.

"Very funny." Searlus managed to pick up some fish meat with the tips of his fingers. He pulled a small bit of flesh off the bone and dropped it into his mouth.

"Disgusting," Navas said. "At least grab a fork or something. No one wants to watch you play with your food."

"You still offering?"

"Offer rescinded," Navas said. "You're just going to starve."

"What a great friend." Searlus pulled some more meat from the bone using his fingers like chop sticks. A drum continued to beat in the background and men continued to sing along with it. Ale flowed freely, but the men stayed somewhat restrained, knowing what lie ahead, and knowing someone would be chosen for first watch. A man with a cloak too tight, hair down to the middle of his back, and a wooden cup full of a honey-colored ale joined them at the table.

"Want me to ask the High Captain if we can turn around so your mommy can dress your wounds?" Kaius asked in a baby voice.

"You've never talked to the High Captain," Navas said before Searlus got a chance. Kaius ignored him.

"It's a long journey, bottom feeders, hope the sea doesn't drive you mad."

"What's your assignment on the *Gildenglory*?" Searlus asked with mock-reverence. Kaius burned his gaze on Searlus before taking a swig of his drink. The commotion of the room was beginning to cease. Kaius stood, leaving his cup on the table.

"It's easy to laugh on the first night at sea. Try to keep your head above the water, Searlus of Ramooth," Kaius said before walking away.

"What was that about?" Navas asked after Kaius had disappeared into the crowd. "Where's he assigned?"

"The *Gomoshah*," Searlus said. "Daddy works with the High Captain and gives the most money to the Lightholm and his kid still got relegated to the third-rate ship."

They both laughed and took another drink of their ale as High Captain Kaphas, Captain Nimrad, and Wayfinder Meeha found their seats at a long table against a far wall of the galley. Searlus knew enough about these voyages to know that this would be the only time these men would eat with them down here. Still, morale was high, and having these men down here to celebrate the last night of the Festival of Floats made it feel like they were just part of the crew. The Saluman officer sat at a small table by himself in the corner of the room.

"Very good," the High Captain said as the last song finished. He clapped his hands. Captain Nimrad did the same. "Very, very good. I always love the first night. Spirits are high, the air is electric, and there's plenty of food." The crew all laughed. Searlus couldn't tell if they're laugher was genuine or from nervousness. "As is our custom on the last night of the festival, Wayfinder Meeha will recount the story of our people. Keep eating. Keep drinking. Enjoy yourselves as you remember." The High Captain nodded to the Wayfinder, who lifted himself from his chair. He brushed the crumbs from his scraggly grey beard and took a drink of wine before clearing his throat.

"We are a sea people. Before the Wavemaker set the land on the seas, he set the boundary of Gildenwood. In Gildenwood he pulled the golden trees from the deep, bursting through the surface and reaching to the skies. He filled this gilded forest with the winged creatures of every kind, with water swimmers of every kind. Wild animals your eyes have never seen swarmed the branches of this forest and the waters below. A river flowed through the forest in Gildenwood. There was no land, for the trees came out of the water. But this was by design. Gildenwood was complete, save for one thing. Humans.

"The Wavemaker gathered up droplets from the sea and made man. Then, he breathed into the nostrils the gale of life and the water being became animate. But the water man was alone. The Wavemaker caught the tears of the first man and formed the first woman. They tended to the forest, the plants, and creatures within. The Wavemaker swam among them. It was good.

"The Wavemaker had told them to drink from anywhere in the forest; to make food from any of the plant life in the forest. But he asked that they not drink from one source, or they would die. In the center of the forest was a still pond where waterlilies dotted the surface in brilliant purples and pinks. In the center of the pond was an incredibly large waterlily whose petals formed a bowl, which held a clear, still water.

"One day a water swimmer led the humans to the

still water. He told them they would not die, but they would become like the Wavemaker. They would live forever and know the ways of the sea. The woman saw that the water was beautiful and mesmerizing and pure, so she drank, and offered some to the man. In that moment the water lily closed in on itself and became a stone. The water swimmer was gone, and the Wavemaker's voice echoed through the trees.

"The humans hid, but the Wavemaker found them, and confronted them. They had to leave. He provided a golden wood watercraft, with a single leather sail, and out of Gildenwood they sailed."

The galley was without sound. The men on board, Captains of the Holy Fleethood, or Captains-in-training, all knew this story by heart. It was the foundation story of their people. But, hearing a Wayfinder share the sacred story was a privilege not many got to experience.

"From there, our ancestors sailed all over these seas. After the great drought, Hakov was a sojourner on the land, and the Wavemaker blessed him and his sons. When the Wavemaker opened the land and our people sailed free from bondage, the Wavemaker was there. When our people established the promised Isles of Hor, and we were a free people, the Wavemaker was there."

Searlus felt a burning sensation in his chest. He sat up straight, forgetting the soreness he brought to dinner. Many of the other crew members leaned forward. Searlus spotted Captain Nimrad staring at the Saluman officer. The Wayfinder continued.

"The whole sea, and the earth within it, is his. And, someday, the Wavemaker will return and establish his kingdom. The boundary of sea and land will be erased. There will be no sun, and no darkness. All will bow their knee to the mighty Mistrider."

The galley erupted with cheers as the crew rose from their seats. Men clapped their hands and yelled. The High Captain sat back and took a drink of his wine, his smile beaming as he raised the cup. After a few cheers of "Horah!" the men settled back down. There were a few whispered conversations finishing up. One of them was between Searlus and Navas.

"You want to make an ass of yourself on the first night?" Navas asked.

"He forgot something," Searlus said louder than he intended. All eyes in the galley were on the only man standing up. Searlus realized his voice echoed off the wooden walls and froze in place. He locked eyes with the High Captain, who studied the young crewmate before speaking.

"Who forgot something?"

"Sit down, Searlus," Navas whispered as he tugged Searlus' cloak. Searlus loosed himself from his friend's grip.

"Nothing, sir," Searlus said as he sat down.

"Come on, son. On this boat, we're family. Enlighten us." Searlus faced his friend and shrugged. Navas dropped his head.

"I was just telling my friend that Wayfinder Meeha forgot to mention the story about old Captain Finnus."

"Tell us," the High Captain commanded.

"Excuse me, sir?" Searlus asked.

"Tell us the story of Captain Finnus."

"Oh," Searlus said. His crewmates had left their food and drink on the table and had given Searlus their undivided attention. Searlus made eye contact with the Wayfinder, and the old man gave a slight smile and a nod. Searlus took a breath. "After the Wavemaker delivered the Horaks from slavery in Agyptos, during the great drift, our ancestors landed upon many islands. On one island, they saw that the women were good, so they brought them on board and took them below the deck.

"This displeased the Wavemaker, for the Horaks had been commanded to not go ashore. Because of this disobedience, storms raged every day after they left the island, and the entire crew became ill. Many died and had to be buried below the waves."

"And Captain Finnus?" the High Captain asked.

"Yes, Captain Finnus. He was faithful to the Wavemaker. One morning, as the ships fought to stay afloat, Captain Finnus took a whaling spear, burst into the sleeping quarters, and caught one of these Horak men in the detestable act. With a jab usually reserved for the hide of a whale, he thrust the spear through the Horak man and the islander. Locking them together forever. That moment, the storm ceased and the illness was lifted."

"And you believe Captain Finnus was correct?" Searlus swallowed as the question hung in the air. He was sure the whole galley heard it. He was only nervous because he was not used to talking in front of so many people. His beliefs were as solid as the pillars of the world.

"I believe in the holy texts, sir," Searlus said. The

High Captain held his stare. Searlus swallowed again. Then, the High Captain started a slow clap before singing the Holy Shanty in his deep voice.

"We sail on the surge of the raging sea..."

It didn't take long for the claps to turn into pounding on the large barrels and the whole crew singing in unison. Searlus joined in the singing and laughing. He looked to Navas, who was still sitting, finishing his meal. Searlus kept singing. He was getting used to this life at sea, and he seemed to be on the High Captain's good side. Things were going well.

And they kept going well, late into the night. It wasn't until the next few days that Searlus would get a healthy dose of reality.

# 7

## TRIGGER WARNING

"It's got to be time," Searlus mumbled. He stood on the bow of the ship and watched the waves come in. The sky was purple like a bruise and Searlus' eyelids were heavier than a barrel filled with wine.

"We've been at sea four days," Navas said.

"It's not that." Searlus dropped his head to the wood rail. "This is the watch from Hadyl."

"The morning hour has gold in its wings," Navas said.

"The afternoon has daylight and warmth. And people. Normal people walking around."

"It's going to be a long voyage."

"And food," Searlus said, ignoring his friend. "The afternoon has food."

"You're not complaining, are you?" Navas asked. Searlus kept his head on the rail, drifting between two worlds. In the dream world, visions of standing high in the crow's nest and being the first to spot Gildenwood warred against the sea-salt slosh of his foot in his boot, reminding him of his rank.

"Would that be the worst thing?"

"Guess not," Navas said. "You could be bawling like a child."

"You can't seriously be enjoying this," Searlus said.

"We're on the open sea," Navas said, with growing bravado. "How many Horaks dream of this opportunity, but never get it?"

Searlus grunted.

"Is it my favorite thing to wake up at the butt-crack break of day to stand on a rolling deck while my feet prune in my boots? Of course not."

"Tell me your ways of happiness, master," Searlus said.

"Perspective. The goal is Gildenwood. And we'd do almost anything to see it. Including the boring stuff. Without the first watch, there's no Gildenwood." Searlus kept his head on the rail and felt the ship rise and fall on the morning waves. The island with golden trees as bright as the sun filled his mind. Navas was right, he'd do anything to see it for himself. He thought that meant fighting tumultuous seas and defending the ship from Zamarians, not forcing himself to stay awake as the sea misted him during the dark morning hours.

The next few days passed in a rhythmic blur. The crew rotated the watch, so Searlus got his wish of being the lookout during the daylight hours. It only took one afternoon standing on the deck with the sun blazing his brow before he realized he preferred the relatively cool mornings. There was no opportunity to rest one's head on the wooden rail of the ship during the afternoon watch. Captain Nimrad patrolled the ship, making sure everything was in order. If he found a man lacking, the punishment would be relegation to cabin boy, or worse.

During an evening watch, Searlus looked over the port side and watched the sun set over the still ocean. Each day he had risen early and wouldn't have a moment of rest until the dark hours of night. Every single day was made up of adjusting sails, up and down, restocking supplies that had fallen from the rise and fall of the sea, and, since Searlus was a carpenter of sorts, repairing the ship. He was surprised how much damage the ship had taken from normal, everyday use.

He'd tell his father he hadn't missed a thing. The most excitement aboard the ship was when two members of the crew got into an argument over the best kind of bread and one of the men crashed into the staircase leading up to the quarterdeck. It was quickly broken up, the men were amiable, and Searlus was pulled from his watch to repair the broken wooden handrail.

There were no rousing dinners, and no grand speeches. It was all work. Every morning and every night. The only respite for Searlus was the moments his watch overlapped with Navas. It was the only time he talked, which meant he'd go days without saying a word. It was one of these evenings a few weeks after leaving the Lightholm, when something happened that shook Searlus from his cloudy stupor. The wind filled the sails as the ship cut through the sea at a steady clip. The men on this watch talked in pairs dotted around the deck. A man laid on a pile of ropes picking his fingernails with a knife. Searlus had his cloak thrown over his knee and was mending it with a needle and thick black thread.

"Have we even moved?" Searlus asked. Navas laughed. "It feels like we're just bobbing up and down like a gull on the beach."

"I heard the crew from last night's watch say they could see the dark outline of the Red Peninsula."

"Put me in a barrel and throw me overboard and I could probably make better time," Searlus said.

"Just trying to match your sewing speed," Navas said. Searlus pulled the needle free and sliced the air near his friend with the tiny sword. Navas shook his head and Searlus turned to see Captain Nimrad leaving the High Captain's quarters. Captain Nimrad surveyed the deck and found the sailor laying on a pile of ropes. The captain marched with his shoulders back toward the man. The sailor saw the second mate coming and jumped to his feet. The other sailors returned to tinkering with the foremast or inspecting the sail.

"Captain Nimrad," the sailor saluted.

"Hasav of Betzun?"

"Yes, sir."

"High Captain Kaphas has requested your transfer to the *Gomoshah* vessel. Effective immediately. Gather your belongings." Hasav stood in silence with a blank look on his face.

"For what reason?"

"The High Captain only accepts the best Horak sailors among the *Gildenglory*. He regrets his mistake in assigning you among this crew."

"You little baby-faced, alley rat—," Hasav shouted,

grabbing hold of Captain Nimrad's cloak. He pulled the man close and looked him in the eye. Captain Nimrad remained as stolid as ever. After a moment, Hasav threw the captain back.

"Looks like you'll be spending a night in the shackles for insubordination," Captain Nimrad said, adjusting his cloak. He turned back toward the High Captain's quarters. Hasav growled and stormed past the second mate, toward the ornate double doors under the quarterdeck. With a violent kick, the doors flew open, revealing the High Captain sitting at a table with the Saluman official. Every sailor awake, including Searlus and Navas, peered into the High Captain's quarters.

"Been serving in the Lightholm near thirty years, I have," Hasav shouted from the open doorway. "Washing every dish that comes down from on high. And this is the thanks I get? Sent to the peasant ship?"

"Oh, right," the High Captain said. "You must be that dishwasher from Betzun. Why are you still on my ship?"

"The Wavemaker ordained this!" Hasav yelled. "You can't take this from me."

"I think I would know what the Wavemaker has or hasn't ordained. Leave."

Hasav rushed toward the High Captain. The Saluman official dodged out of the way as the Horak sailor flipped the table into the air. The next moment, a glint of steel flashed in the air. Hasav froze in place. The High Captain was standing with his arm outstretched. The cold tip of his revolver rested on Hasav's oily forehead.

"Nimrad," the High Captain said as if he was calling for tea. "Take this man to the brig."

"Yes, sir," Captain Nimrad said, entering the room and grabbing the man by the arms. "For how long, sir?"

"As long as the Wavemaker ordains."

# 8

## ALL PRAISE

A few days later, during Searlus' first watch, the *Gomoshah* was tethered to the *Gildenglory* and a man with his arms bound behind his back was led up from deep below deck and onto the smaller ship. There were no harsh words. No yelling. There was only a man accepting his fate.

The whole crew had swapped their versions of the story until Searlus heard two young cooks telling how the High Captain shot the sailor three times and nearly killed him. Searlus didn't blame the lads, as it was the most exciting thing to happen up to that point, and it was still the most exciting thing that had happened since. But, that was not what kept Searlus' spirits high.

Navas had been right. They were making progress.

They sailed north and strips of land lined the horizon in both the east and west. Soon they would cross Octav's Channel. Which meant they would get a glimpse of Salumoor.

Searlus had never been to Salumoor. He'd never even

seen it in the distance. The closest thing he got to the city was his barrels. Every few months a Saluman tax collector would come through Tarsa and collect a tax from the citizens. King Tiveros loved to drink, which meant the palace needed many oak barrels. Navas had worked a deal in which a handful of the best barrels would satisfy the tax. He was excited to see the place where his workmanship had been sent, even if it was from a distance.

"Wake up, Searlus," Navas said, shaking his friend.

"I'm third watch," Searlus said.

"Salumoor." With that single word, Searlus jumped out of bed, pulled on the same cloak he'd worn since he first boarded the ship, and followed his friend up to the main deck. It was the end of the first watch, but the whole crew had received the news and had flooded the bow, all looking toward the east.

The land was near as they prepared to pass through Octav's Channel and they could make out the shapes of the mountains in the twilight. The Great River ran through the valley of the mountains all the way to the sea. At the mouth of the river stood a giant stone eagle with its wings spread wide and its talons extended. The base of the statue was submerged and the water flowed around it. Searlus had heard stories about the massive statue. It served as a warning for any who tried to enter Salumoor via the river.

"Take in the sails!" Captain Nimrad said, and like a trained hound, the crew went to work. Searlus grabbed hold of the ropes securing the foresail and began loosening it up. A few men grabbed the main sail and did the same. The sun had risen just over the mountains as the *Gildenglory* came to a near stop in the shadow of the stone eagle. That's when Searlus saw it.

Salumoor.

The river was a street of silver leading to the greatest city in the world. The sun reflected off of the many golden spired buildings. Systematic holes were carved into the mountain, which Searlus guessed were homes. The palace rose highest of all in the middle of the city, making Salumoor look like a small mountain in the bowl of the actual mountains. The whole crew stood in silence as they took it in. Even those who had made the voyage in years past never tired of seeing the spectacle.

The trance was broken only by the sound of the High Captain's door opening. The men fumbled their way back to work but were interrupted by the High Captain's soothing voice.

"Men," he said as he approached the bow. The Saluman officer was close behind, carrying a small pouch. "Take it in. Rest from your work this moment. It is the great city of Salumoor. There is nothing like it." The men turned back to the city, but some eyed the Saluman official. The High Captain nodded to Captain Nimrad who gave orders to a few sailors. They went below deck and returned with a small wooden platform. They placed it at the front of the ship and faded back into the crew's ranks. The High Captain nodded to the Saluman official, who promptly ascended the single step up onto the platform.

"Great King Tiveros, there is none like you. From the gods you have descended. From the gods you are. Among mere mortals you dwell. Do protect me this day, and the next."

Though the sea was calm, and the air crisp, the atmosphere on the ship was tense. The Horak sailors shifted nervously as the blasphemous claims were being made. For the Horaks, the Wavemaker was the only supreme being. Any other claim to transcendence was an affront to the Wavemaker, as the Horaks knew firsthand. Their history was littered with their people being seduced by the deities of the land.

Once the Saluman official had finished his desecration of the ship, he dropped to his knees and held the pouch out over the sea. He slipped a knife from his waist and slit the bottom of the bag, spilling gold coins into the sea. The moment the last coin fell, a slight current passed and shifted the deck, causing the Saluman official to lurch forward. He dropped the bag and the knife, trying to free his hands to catch his balance, but failed. The sailors heard a splash.

"Man overboard!" Captain Nimrad said. A few sailors grabbed a nearby rope, tied a loop, and tossed it over the rail. A few other men went to the stern and returned with a rope ladder. They secured it to the side of the ship and tossed it over. Searlus mustered as much restraint as he could to keep from laughing. He saw poorly concealed smiles on the faces of his fellow crew mates. He had to turn away when the Saluman official pulled himself over the rail and back onto the ship, hair matted to the side of his face, clothes hanging low with the burden of saltwater.

"This changes nothing," the Saluman official said to

the High Captain. He was pointing at the raised wooden platform that had become his diving board.

"Of course. Prepare the sacrifice," the High Captain said to Captain Nimrad.

The mood on the deck changed in a moment as the crew realized what was being asked of their High Captain. Searlus, like the rest of the crew, knew what the Wavemaker required of them. This direct offence could subject them to the Wavemaker's wrath for the rest of their journey, leading to illness, storms, and even death. Searlus opened his mouth to say something but closed it almost right away. He did it again. He knew someone had to say something. The third time he opened his mouth to speak, Captain Nimrad made his way to the main deck with three Horaks behind him.

Two men held the largest tarpon Searlus had ever seen. The massive fish, taller than any man on board, squirmed in their grip. Searlus had heard there was a live well in the kitchen, which the chef used to cook the High Captain fresh meals. The last man in line struggled to carry a large stone with a rope tied around it. The crew watched as if they were part of a funeral procession.

The High Captain removed his outer light blue cloak and handed it to Captain Nimrad before rolling his sleeves and approaching the wooden platform. The rock was set on the platform, and the fish handed to the High Captain. By the look on the faces of the crew, they watched with disgust or confusion as the High Captain got to his knees on the edge of the ship, with a sacrifice in hand, facing Salumoor.

"Look upon us this morning, holy Wavemaker. Hear

our plea. You are supreme. Accept this offering on behalf of King Tiveros. May it be pleasing to you."

With the final words, just like the Saluman official had done, the High Captain pulled a knife from his waist and slit the fish from mouth to tail. Blood spilled onto the wood. He secured the rope around the fish corpse, pulling it tight, before using his hands, dripping red, to push the stone overboard. His sacrifice hit the sea with a hollow thump.

The High Captain rose to his feet and stared out toward Salumoor. After a moment, he descended the step and washed his hands in a basin Captain Nimrad had provided. The Saluman official, still dripping on the deck, met the High Captain's eyes. The rest of the crew was frozen in place. The only sound came from the gulls posturing on the shore, fighting for food.

The next moment, the Saluman official nodded and returned to his quarters below deck. Captain Nimrad shouted, "Full sail ahead!"

# 9

## OPEN SEA

The sacrifice for the King of Salumoor was the talk of the ship for the following days. In the dark corners of the ship, the young sailors whispered worries while the elder spoke harsh criticisms. The boys feared the Wavemaker would not look kindly on the High Captain's gesture, and that their fate on this voyage was doomed. The old men despised the High Captain for what they considered a long line of appeasing the Saluman Empire, and not holding fast to the Horak tradition.

But, like all gossip and spectacle aboard a ship, the monotony of the sea swallowed all interest after a few short days. The men aboard the ship had come aware of a threat much more urgent. They had entered the rough waters of the Sea of Beasts.

Most Horak captains had sailed up to Octav's Channel, and all around the Ruby Sea. The last part of their training to become a captain in the Holy Fleethood was to make a solo voyage in a small vessel around the Ruby Sea. They would sail to landmarks from their histories.

The Sea of Beasts was different. No one crossed Octav's Channel, especially not solo. There was nothing out there, except for Gildenwood, which existed on the horizon of legend for most Horaks. The only other legends living in this vast water expanse were those that dwelt below the surface.

Tales of fish as big as a ship and squid with eyes like the moon were told to the Horak children to keep them from sailing too far. Searlus had heard all of the stories. He'd read the holy texts and knew these great beasts were subject to the Wavemaker. He was old enough now to know which stories had been exaggerated to keep seafaring children at bay. And, seeing how this was his first time upon the Sea of Beasts, he had never encountered a water dweller bigger than a rowboat.

That would soon change.

Searlus' turn to take the morning watch had come yet again and he found himself thinking of his sister as he aired out two long linen sheets used as tablecloths in the High Captain's chambers. He remembered the light in her eyes, and how they contrasted the dark rings below. Devora claimed it was because she'd been hanging out with the new magician in town. It was all trouble in Searlus' eyes. Men had come before doing tricks. Claiming to be the Mistrider or one like him. Many even gathered a small following of radicals. But that is what they always were.

Radicals.

The Horak radicals that followed these insurrectionists always ended up murdered by the empire, like their deranged leaders. King Tiveros gained the throne through spilling blood. Blood of his own family. He did not think twice of squashing any Horak rebellion. Searlus feared his sister would share the same fate of those before.

He prayed a dirge to the Wavemaker, one of his favorites from the holy texts. He prayed the Wavemaker would guide their sails among rightly currents. When he finished his prayer he opened his eyes and looked out upon the glassy sea. Light filled the sky, but the sun had not crossed the threshold into this new day. The pink sky contrasted the dark waters. It wasn't the wonderful pastels of first morning that caught Searlus' attention. He stared into the waters at the edge of his vision.

No, not the waters. Something in the waters. Something piercing the surface of the deep. Something they were sailing directly toward.

As best as Searlus could tell, the trunk of a lone tree waved wildly in the distance. Searlus stood up straight to get a better view, but it wasn't enough. Without thinking it through, he grabbed hold of a nearby rope and climbed up to the rail of the ship. Though they sailed along at a steady pace, from his perch on the rail, he nearly became a fourth sail on the *Gildenglory*. The tails of his cloak flailed in the wind, forcing him to work hard to keep his balance.

His heightened viewpoint accompanied by the

distance they'd covered since he first spotted the mysterious object allowed him to see with a bit more clarity. That was all he needed.

"Captain Nimrad!" Searlus said as he jumped down from the rail. The other Horak sailors looked at Searlus with dreary annoyance. It was the end of a long watch, and the unspoken rule was that quiet hours were still in effect. None of that mattered to Searlus. They were sailing toward something massive. This is what the watch was for.

He knew Captain Nimrad would not be about the deck at this hour, so he descended into the belly of the ship toward the first mate's quarters. He stumbled down the last stair and fell onto the wooden door. He knocked frantically. After a moment the door creaked open and Captain Nimrad stood in full Horak regalia, looking like he hadn't slept at all.

"Someone better be dying," Captain Nimrad sneered.

"In the waters," Searlus said. "Something in the waters."

"A ship?" Captain Nimrad asked, his voice nearly cracking.

"No sir." He knew it would sound ridiculous, but the crew was in danger. "A beast, sir."

The first mate closed his eyes for a moment and gave Searlus a look he had not seen since he was a boy, when his father had been frustrated with his incompetence in the woodshop. Captain Nimrad looked up and said, "Go on, then. Show me."

Searlus turned and made his way back up the stairs

toward the deck. Captain Nimrad followed behind. The sun had begun its ascent over the horizon, which meant the deck was bathed in golden light. Every sailor stared in confusion as Searlus led the first mate to the bow of the ship.

"Out there," Searlus said. "It was like an arm or something moving above the water." The first mate pulled a brass spy glass from inside his cloak and extended it toward the sea. He scanned the waters for any irregularities. With his naked eye, Searlus scanned the waters for the object, but found nothing. After a few moments, the first mate retracted the spy glass and returned it to its proper place. Searlus spoke before the first mate had a chance.

"It was there," Searlus said. "I saw it."

"This is the Sea of Beasts," Captain Nimrad said, voice as cool as the breeze that carried the ship. "And for good reason. Might have been a repulsive beast from the depths of Hadyl or it could have been your eyes playing tricks on you."

"I saw it," Searlus said to himself, trying to convince himself more than the first mate.

"Sound the alarm if it really is something. No shame in that. But you better be sure."

"Yes, sir," Searlus said, looking down at the damp wood planks below his feet.

"Back to your watch."

...

During the next few days, Searlus spent his limited

free time looking over the rail of the ship. He studied the dark waters for any sign of life. Late one afternoon Searlus and Navas had a rare moment of downtime. They met on the bow, Searlus holding onto the rail looking out over the sea, and Navas sitting on the deck, with his back against the foremast.

"Ninety gold," Navas said. "Can you believe that?"

"We'd be lucky to see that after running the shop our whole lives," Searlus said. Navas got quiet. Searlus felt the awkward silence growing but was unaware of what caused it. Still, he didn't turn from the sea to face his friend. Navas changed the subject.

"Your dad didn't show when we set sails, did he?"

"No," Searlus said.

"Sorry to hear that," Navas said. "At least you've got a dad."

"Not again," Searlus said in jest. "Parents stood up for some Horak refugees. Killed by Saluman guards. Little Navas is orphaned at age five. I've heard it a thousand times."

"And you'll hear it a thousand more," Navas said. "You might not be seeing eye to eye with your folks, but at least they've got eyes you can look in."

"I guess I'm a lesser man, then," Searlus said. "Been more than one time I've thought about sailing across the bay and starting a new life in the mountains of Golaun. Devora's the only thing that's got me staying."

"I'm touched," Navas said. "All jokes aside, I wouldn't go anywhere she wasn't either."

"Ah, back off," Searlus said. He lifted his boot and gave Navas a little shove. "I think she's in real trouble these days." Navas pulled himself up from the deck and stood next to his friend.

"She's a grown woman, Searlus, she can take care of herself. Remember when she stowed away on-board that two-master?"

"This seems different. That was kid stuff. Seems like she really believes this magician. The empire could squash this cult before we even get back."

"The Wavemaker won't let that happen," Navas said.

"How can you, of all people, say something like that?"

"That's where we're different. You think the Wavemaker has failed if he doesn't come down and smite someone. I know if I've still got the salty air in my lungs, he's working."

"Tell him to hurry up, then," Searlus said. "I'm tired of being Saluman slaves. We're citizens, too. The Isles of Hor were ours first."

"That we can agree on. Each day I hope will be the day the Wavemaker looses the grip of the Saluman Empire from around our necks. Between you and me, the day is coming. I think it's coming soon."

Searlus opened his mouth to reply to his friend's hopeful prophecy, but his voice dried up when his gaze caught something far in the distance. Dusk was only just settling upon them, and the whole sea glowed with golden light. Searlus blinked his eyes before focusing in on the object again. He grabbed his friend's arm.

"Tell me you see that," he said as he pointed over the rail. Navas peered out across the sea, head on a swivel, until he froze in place. "You see it?" Searlus asked, growing impatient. Navas nodded his head. Searlus bounded across the deck toward the High Captain's quarters. But, before he could reach it, he heard the call ring out from the crow's nest high above.

"Zamarian ship inbound!"

# 10
## FULL SAIL

In a blink, the *Gildenglory* sprung to life. Men flooded out from below deck. Sailors ran frantically from foremast to mizzenmast. Among the chaos, the High Captain strode out from his quarters, and seemed to walk in slow motion to the bow. He pulled a spyglass from his belt, opposite of the revolver, and extended it toward the horizon. The crew slowed their pace, waiting for the next command. The High Captain talked low with his first mate. A moment later, the first mate yelled out, so even the crew of the *Noak Tava* and *Gomoshah* could hear.

"Full sail ahead!"

The crew continued moving about the ship with frantic energy, but now that the command had been made, there was a sense of ordered chaos as the men scrambled to their stations. Searlus ran toward the front of the ship and uncoiled the rope keeping the flying jib rolled up. As he released the flying jib, it filled with wind. The other smaller sails had been loosed, and Searlus could feel the ship gaining speed. The High Captain had made his way to helm. In an attempt to catch as much of the wind as possible, the High Captain spun the wheel violently causing the ship to turn to the northeast, setting them off their course.

Searlus tied off his rope and scanned the ship to map out his next course of action, and his eyes landed on an area that was unattended.

A cannon.

He shuffled down the three stairs from the bow to the unattended weapon and began untying the ropes which secured it to the rail. As he performed the same action with the rope that he had just done with the sail, unwinding it around in a reverse figure eight, he wondered why no one had been here yet. In his mind, cannon preparations should have begun at first sight of the black flag.

"Stop," a tender voice called out behind him. Searlus felt a hand on his shoulder. He turned and found a somewhat familiar face. It was the first crew member he had met, way back in the bay surrounding the Lightholm, when the crews were selected. Captain Hemol wore a wispy gray beard and looked as frail as a windsock. Still, for some reason, the Wavemaker had chosen him to be part of the crew.

"Zamarians," Searlus said, pointing out over the sea.

"They are not our enemy," Captain Hemol said. Just then, three thunderclaps rolled in rhythmic succession. Splashes erupted from the water in a similar pattern, like a trio of whales exhausting their spiracle.

"They just fired at us," Searlus said a little louder.

"You know the Zamarian lineage, yes?"

"They just fired at us!" Searlus said again.

"They are sons of Hakov too. They live on the remote coasts of Hevraun. Part of our sacred Isles."

"They'll kill us."

"Cannons are a last resort," Captain Hemol said. "Help secure the deck." The old captain walked away before Searlus could speak again. Searlus angled the cannon out over the sea, toward the multicolored ship. The Zamarian hull had so many replaced boards it looked like a patchwork rug. Searlus pretended to strike a match against the side of the steel cannon and light the fuse.

"Boom," he whispered as he imagined the steel ball crashing into the foremast, taking down the main sail. The ball continued through the foremast and into the main deck, through the lower levels, and out the bottom of the hull. Within minutes the ocean had swallowed the ship up. Searlus was being hoisted in the air by the crew, and the High Captain appointed him as the new first mate.

"Get your hands on this net," someone near him said. Searlus was shaken from his daydream and found the Zamarian ship still in pursuit, and the steel cannon cold before him. Members of the crew scrambled behind him. Some hauled crates below deck. Others continued to secure lines. The man nearest to him was struggling with a loose net sprawled out on the damp deck. "I said get your chicken footed self over here, boy."

Searlus sprang into action.

He grabbed the opposite end of the sea-soaked net and helped the man wrangle it. In the short time since the warning rang out, the deck had been cleared of any excess. Searlus assumed it had been taken below in case the Zamarians got close enough to board the *Gildenglory*. There would be more room to hold them off, and the Zamarians would have a harder time getting to the plunder.

Searlus and the grumpy captain who had called for help had nearly finished stowing the net under the stairs leading to the helm when the High Captain disengaged from the wheel and stood on the balcony over the deck.

"I have no doubt that we would make short work of the Zamarian wretches. We outnumber them three to one. The mere thought of letting those mule-faced bastards vandalize the *Gildenglory* turns me red within."

The High Captain paused to regain his composure. The crew began to mumble to each other about what the next step would be. More Horaks emerged from below deck to hear the High Captain's orders.

"We sail on. Their kind do not have the patience for a long pursuit. By morning they will have abandoned course, and their sails will be a mite of dust on the horizon."

A hearty "Horah" erupted around Searlus. The crew seemed content with this plan. They went back to their posts and the tension seemed to dissolve in the newfound breeze their speed created. Searlus eyed the ship in the distance and felt a knot forming in his stomach. The High Captain was not to be questioned, but there was one thing that couldn't be denied.

The Zamarian ship was getting closer.

. . .

Darkness fell over the waters, and the bouncing orange firelight was all that could be seen trailing behind them. They were still on full alert, and the crew moved like ghosts among the decks. Captain Hemol paced the deck, murmuring something under his breath.

The line leading to the lower mizen top sail had snapped near midnight. The untethered sail flung wildly in the moonlight. Searlus couldn't feel any noticeable effects from the lost sail, but he knew their speed had decreased slightly. He kept glancing back and forth from the fire on the horizon to the Horaks assigned to scale the mizen mast and tend to the sail.

By the time the morning came around, the damaged sail had been removed from its rigging, and had been taken below deck to be mended. Captain Hemol continued his pacing, murmuring. Each member of the crew leaned against anything solid, standing against anything that could give them a brief respite. The Zamarian ship continued in its pursuit, and more details of the ship came into sharp focus.

The Zamarian crew jumped up and down with wild abandon. They yelled and screamed profanities. Their bodies had been painted all shades of whites and blacks. Derogatory claims that Zamarians were less than human found their grounding in the actions of the crew in pursuit.

Many of the young Horaks, Searlus included, were mesmerized by the barbaric display. The screams and growls, carried by the wind, accomplished its goal once it reached the deck of the *Gildenglory*. The young seamen fidgeted about, mumbling to each other. Searlus tapped his hand on the wooden rail in a sporadic cadence. Despite all the showmanship, the Zamarians were only partially responsible for the uneasiness of the Horak crew.

Dark clouds gathered directly ahead of them. The infernal billows covered the entire sky. Lightning flashed in the distance. Thunder rumbled, mixing with the booms of the cannons from behind. Searlus scanned the deck for Navas, wanting some source of comfort, but he was nowhere to be found. The cook had discovered Navas' natural talent in the culinary arts and had recruited him to help prepare meals. The two friends saw each other less and less as each nautical night passed. And now Searlus was alone.

"Looks a nasty one," a raspy voice said behind him. Searlus turned from the gathering storm and found a familiar face. Captain Hemol's golden sun pendant was muted from the overcast skies.

"We haven't changed course," Searlus said.

"Sometimes you can see the storms coming. Sometimes you can't." Captain Hemol joined Searlus at the rail. "Either way, doesn't make facing them any easier."

"Death by scoundrels or death by sea," Searlus said in a daze.

"The Wavemaker will make a way," Captain Hemol said with the same soothing certainty which he always spoke. "We'll lose the Zamarians in the storm. Their lack of faith will force them to retreat."

"Death by sea, then," Searlus said to himself. Captain Hemol let out a faint laugh. A cold droplet stung Searlus on the nape of his neck. He pulled his cloak up instinctively. He heard the soft pattering as more tiny cannonballs pelted the deck. The dark clouds were overhead now. A moment later the High Captain appeared on the helm. The entire crew stood at attention with fearful expectation.

"Full sail ahead!" High Captain Kaphas yelled. "Into the storm."

# II

## STORMS

The Zamarians had started the wide arc of a hundred and eighty degree turn at the first streak of lightning overhead. Their tattered sails and black flag had disappeared, but the Horak crew didn't notice. As darkness surrounded the three Horak ships and thick sheets of rain drenched them, each of their crews began bracing for the storm ahead.

Swift gusts of wind swept over every inch of the ship. Waves crashed onto the wooden deck as the sea tried to claim another trophy. Rain pelted Searlus' face at an angle, rendering his cloak useless. The rambunctious scurrying of the crew at the first sight of the Zamarians turned out to be just a foretaste of dire panic as more men flooded the deck, hauling ropes and buckets, replacing sails, securing the safety lines around the rail, and giving the sloshing sea back to herself.

"No sign of the *Gomoshah*," Searlus heard a voice call from the helm.

"I've lost the *Noak Tava*," a voice said in reply. Searlus popped his head out from his work uncoiling a rope and surveyed the rolling waves. The three ships had been sailing as a uniform triumvirate, with the *Gildenglory* leading the way. The chase from the Zamarians had caused them to pull their ranks tighter to support each other in case the Zamarians closed the gap. As the storm hit, Searlus assumed these sister ships were still nearby. Fear dropped like a smoldering coal in his chest when he discovered how fast an angry sea could separate three large vessels.

Just then a rogue wave crashed down onto the forecastle deck, knocking Searlus from his feet. His back cracked against the damp wood, knocking the wind out of him. Darkness covered his vision. There was no telling if his eyes were open or closed.

"Get up," the shadow of a man said and he pulled Searlus to his feet. Searlus stumbled toward the side of the ship, just catching the rail. His momentum carried the top half of his body over the deadly sea, but his carpenter hands held firm, keeping him planted on the ship. A flash of lightning cut the sky, and what Searlus saw floating in the water sobered him up in an instant.

A dark mass broke the surface of the water and rose toward the ship like a cursed tree from Hadyl.

"Beast!" Searlus said over the roar of the storm. The Horaks nearby were already frozen in their soaked boots as three other coils surrounded the bow of the ship. The dark mass of the coils danced against the infernal sky, mesmerizing Searlus and those nearby. Then, without warning, the arms of the Coiled Whale crashed down onto the deck, crushing the rail beneath. The safety lines snapped and flailed wildly in the chaos.

A high-pitched trumpet squealed a single note of alarm. Moments later a dozen men burst onto the deck from below carrying swords. Searlus ran toward the men, to flee the beast and to give himself space to unsheathe the sword at his waist. The first wave of Horak captains ran past Searlus and toward the tentacles clinging to the ship.

A new sound had joined chaotic symphony. Steel swords hacked away at the fleshy beast with muted bloody thud after muted bloody thud. An empty mess of splintered wood was all that remained where the leftmost tentacle had struck. The first wave of attackers had begun work on the remaining two tentacles. As Searlus neared, he saw the Horak frontline was made of the oldest captains. Among them was Captain Hemol, who hacked away at the beast with what looked like a personal vendetta.

Searlus joined the crew slicing the middle tentacle. In the repeated flash of lightning Searlus could see the bulging muscle of the Coiled Whale as it held its grip on the foremast. Searlus sliced downward on the flesh, but when the deck was illuminated with lightning, it looked as if he'd done no damage. The torrential rain washed any blood away immediately. Searlus wondered if the beast felt anything more than what he felt when a piece of a barrel splintered his palm.

Still, he slashed with reckless abandon. It was the first task in his life that he had undertaken with singular focus, for he knew that his efforts, along with his Horak brothers, would result in life or death. After a few moments of sustained attack, the Horak efforts were accompanied by an unexpected ally.

A wall of water crashed down onto the bow, knocking the crew off their feet. Searlus cleared the salty sea from his face, and through blurred darkness was relieved to find the ghastly appendage which he had attacked had been loosed by the wave. His triumph was short-lived as he eyed the remaining tentacle keeping the *Gildenglory* firm in its grasp.

All about the ship men yelled at each other, yelled at themselves, and yelled at the Wavemaker. Three or four more bulbous tentacles rose out of the rolling deep, swaying back and forth in the storm. The beast was preparing for a deathly hug, and once the *Gildenglory* was in its grip, it would dive down, down, down to Hadyl, bringing her crew along.

Searlus put those thoughts out of his mind. His task remained clear before him. He had kept hold of his sword after the wave crashed, and now he got to his feet, preparing to sever the grip of the Coiled Whale on the ship. Before he could get there, a shadowy figure yelled, "He shall slay the dragon from the deep," and charged the beast with sword raised. He brought the sword down with a two-handed vengeance, tearing a deep gash in the fishy flesh. The tentacle loosened its grip, but not without repercussion.

In an instant, the tentacle swept across the deck like a boulder rolling down a mountain. Captain Hemol was the only Horak who had regained his footing and was standing near the arm of the beast. Just as fast as he had sliced his steel through the beast, the beast had responded by sweeping its arm and pulling Captain Hemol into the sea.

"No!" Searlus said but could hardly hear his own yell above the riotous scene he could not escape. He rushed to the side of the ship, looking over the broken rail into the abysmal sea for any sign of his Horak brother. Only sea and foaming sea filled his vision. A loud splintering rang out overhead.

"The foresail!" a voice called out behind him. The white cloth fluttered in the storm like the last leaf holding on to a tree in late autumn. A rope that helped secure the foresail flailed wildly nearby like a flying snake. Instinctively, for it doesn't take long on the deck of a ship to acquire new instincts to survive the life at sea, Searlus sheathed his sword and sprang into action.

The ship rocked back and forth beneath his feet, and the soaking wet deck caused him to lose his footing more than once. But, as he neared the foremast he leapt into the air and wound his right hand around the rope, holding it tight. His weight carried him toward the deck, but just as his toe touched the wood, a wild gale blew up and filled the sail. The rope retracted and Searlus flew into the air. He swung helplessly as he rose higher up the foremast. With an abruptness that nearly made him lose his grip, he jerked to a halt halfway to the crow's nest.

The rope had jammed in the pulley.

The sea rocked the boat, swinging him back and forth, from port side to starboard like the clapper of a bell. He twisted and spun as he swung, but he dared not let go for fear of crashing into the deck and breaking his legs. Or worse, falling into the sea.

He managed to look down, but it was a moment when only the sea was below. Again, lightning filled the sky and Searlus saw the dark silhouette of the Coiled Whale with its body the size of the *Gildenglory* and its arms unfurling like a black widow about to eat a fly.

A thunder crack like a hammer to the skull rang in Searlus' ears. The thunder thus far had been a steady roll like the drumbeats of an approaching parade. But this was different, and Searlus had no time to brace himself for the auditory attack. Despite withstanding the weeks at sea, the looming Zamarian attack, the turbulent seas, and the tentacles of the Coiled Whale, the sound of the Wavemaker's gong proved too much for him.

His hand slipped from the rope, and he crashed into the sea.

# 12

## WRAPPED UP

It was impossible for Searlus to know in the moment, though he would find out shortly, that his hand had slipped from the rope only because the previously taut rope had become slack in his grip. This slackness was due to the fraying and eventual snapping of the rope near the pulley. So, as Searlus plunged into the wet void, so did the rope which had delayed his fate.

He crashed into the water with a sting, his back breaking his fall. His cloak had been soaked by the torrential rain, but the submersion brought complete saturation. Whereas some remote parts of his being had previously retained splotched dryness, with his dive into the sea, his whole being had been soaked through.

The silence was more jarring than the cold wetness. Chaos sounds from the deck were muted in an almost peaceful hum. His subconscious reflex propelled him above the surface of the water in search of air. His head broke the surface and he gulped down a deep breath as he felt something settling on his shoulders, restricting the movement of his arms.

His head dipped below the surface as his arms were restricted by the rope. It coiled around him as if it were alive with malicious intent. The sounds from above faded away as the ocean pulled him down. Fighting the tangled ropes seemed to cause them to tighten their grip even more.

His mind went clear in an instant.

He would never see his sister in this world again. And if his sister was involved with a cult that opposed the Wavemaker, he wouldn't see her at the end of time when the Wavemaker restored his people. Searlus kicked wildly. Thoughts of his apathy toward his sister's choices caused hot guilt to well up inside of him. The guilt turned to anger and rage and he flailed about more violently.

He knew his parents would remain faithful, and that he'd see them again. There was a moment of peace as he pictured his mother waving to him as he departed on this journey. He hated that the last time he'd seen his father was when he left in a fury. He kicked about again, angry that he hadn't sought out his father again, and angry that his father hadn't shown at the departure.

A wave of exhaustion washed over his body. The ropes held their captive tight, but Searlus felt his shoulders roll back and his arms float freely in their restraints. He forced his eyes open in vain with hopes that blurred vision would assist him, but what he saw proved to drown any hope of rescue.

As he scanned his surroundings, a flash of lightning struck overhead yet again. Searlus saw the rope woven around his body, but out in the deep water, a mass floated silently in the void under the ship. The otherworldly darkness of the Coiled Whale silhouetted the dark sea. Eight tentacles waved back and forth with an ominous, slow cadence. One moved toward Searlus.

Just like men and women from time immemorial who seek a divine intervention in the face of impending death, Searlus cried out a warbled prayer to the Wavemaker. Salt water stung his tongue as he began crying out. His mind was the clearest it had ever been.

*I'll do whatever you ask of me. Let me live.*

He sank, singularly focused on his request, and mouthed that he would never doubt the Wavemaker again and would serve him relentlessly if only he was saved from this moment.

The silent prayer bubbled up to the surface and was gone.

A growing pressure filled his ears as he continued to sink. He mouthed his oath over and over. His thrashing grew weaker and weaker, yet the grip of the rope grew tighter and tighter. With every repetition of his prayer, a part of his body succumbed to the inevitable. His arms ceased their attempted escape and floated against the rope. He shut his eyes to face the eternal darkness.

But, just as his legs slowed from their kick, something solid and cold brushed against his thigh. His eyes shot open once again. Panic exploded from his chest out to his arms and legs. He tried to kick and shove, but the tentacle of the Coiled Whale squeezed even tighter. His prayers turned to screams suffocated with salt water. The beast had him in its grip.

The tentacle began to move Searlus through the water at an increasing speed. Searlus' mind was still fraught with terror, but in a glimpse of clarity, he realized the beast was not pulling him down to the depths of Hadyl. Before the next thought had fully formed he burst through the surface of the rolling waves.

Searlus gasped for breath and took countless small gulps of air trying to steady himself. Raindrops resumed their assault on his face. As his mind cleared, he realized two things, one which brought him relief; and one which shook him to his bones. To his relief, the rope had fallen from around his body during the ascent. He kicked his feet and circled his arms effortlessly to keep himself afloat.

The terror came as he spun himself in the water, surveying the sea around him. The *Gildenglory* was nowhere to be found. Only billowing, blue-black sea and thunderous sky filled his vision in every direction.

"I'm not saved yet!" Searlus said with a hollow breath, thinking on the oath he'd prayed below the surface. He repeated variations of his indignation as he bobbed above the waves until something struck his back. Searlus yelled again, but this time in terror, fearing the Coiled Whale or some other nefarious sea beast. What he found was something quite comforting and familiar.

A wooden barrel, one that he and Navas had fashioned specifically for the journey to Gildenwood, floated alongside him. He reached his arms around it in full embrace, like it was an estranged prodigal come home, and it bore his weight and kept him afloat.

Relief which had been absent the last few days now

rushed over him. His adrenaline had run dry, and a deep tiredness filled his mind and body. On the verge of exhaustion, he managed to tuck part of his cloak into the metal band around the barrel, securing himself to his life raft before passing out.

# 13
## THE OATH

The skin on his face felt stretched like a canvas. Even before he had regained consciousness he was aware of the stark contrast between his dust-dry head and his soggy legs and feet. All signs of storm and turmoil had passed and a cloudless sky hung overhead. Impossibly bright sunlight painted his exposed face. He wasn't sure which was worse, the incessant raindrops or the relentless sun rays.

Searlus' first instinct, before he'd even opened his eyes, was to check his neck. The gold pendant still hung from his neck. Next, he pulled his cloak back over his head. It was damp from hanging in the sea while he remained unconscious, but it brought a welcome relief to the heat. He tugged on the bit of his cloak which had served as his lifeline from the barrel.

Next, he checked his body for any injuries. His toes and feet all seemed fine, albeit waterlogged. He patted down his stomach and chest, simultaneously checking for broken ribs or broken fingers. A sharp pain pierced his side. He moved on gingerly to his neck, feeling his scar, then onto his head, where he found a laceration above his eye.

All in all, a broken rib and a forehead cut meant he'd survived a storm at sea, being thrown overboard, and encountering a Coiled Whale firsthand, all while remaining relatively unscathed. Despite his good fortune, thoughts of gratitude for his good fortune did not fill his mind.

He looked out at the sea again, just as he'd done in darkness the night before, and found an illuminated version of his misfortunes. No ship, or land, or any living thing could be found. His hand brushed his hip and his anger grew. His grandfather's blade was gone. Torn from his side by the sea or the beast. Forever lost to the depths of Hadyl. The anger he'd inherited from his father, hotter than the scorching rays, welled up inside of him.

Curses followed.

"No!" was all he could articulate at first. "No! No! No!"

He dropped his head on the barrel. The saltwater stung his open head wound. He didn't care. It only reminded him of the unfulfilled oath. Images of home, his sister, the *Gildenglory*, Navas, and the Lightholm flooded his mind in rapid succession, and with no discernable continuity. They were gone. It was only the ocean and his barrel now. These thoughts lit a new fuse inside of him.

"Curse you!" he cried out to the sky. "This is not saving. Deliver me! I made an oath!"

There was no response, save the rhythmic quieting of the waves.

...

Searlus' life had devolved into a pattern of curse, sleep, repeat. When he was awake, he floated along on his barrel, screaming curses, and damning the Wavemaker for his current misfortunes. This would last until he passed out from exhaustion and heat. Sleep would overtake him for a few hours, until a rogue wave washed over him, jolting him from his trance, or his face began to sting from the sun cooking his skin. Then, he'd wake and start the cycle again.

He woke, after one particularly long rest, and found himself in complete darkness. The sky remained clear, and the moon illuminated the water like a candle in a forest. Stars blanketed the sky with divine splendor. Searlus was not in a place to take in any of the beauty surrounding him. This time, however, it wasn't anger that blinded him, it was terror.

Visions of being tossed overboard replayed in his mind. He tried to keep his eyes open to keep the visions from playing back, but it was no help. Worst of all, the silhouette of the Coiled Whale floating in front of him made him gasp for air. He checked the water below him every other moment and jumped nearly out of the water when the tail of his cloak brushed up against his calf.

Hour after hour passed, and instead of sleeping, Searlus spent his time scanning the surrounding sea. At one point, he swore he saw the faint glow of a luneshark far below the surface. It turned out to be a reflection from a particularly bright star.

Later, he saw a dark, inky mass moving up the water toward him. He screamed and abandoned his barrel, swimming as far away as possible. He was reminded of his physical exhaustion after a few strokes and slowed his pace until he was floating, alone in the dark, wet expanse. Moments passed and no infernal beast breached the surface to consume him, so he swam gently back toward his barrel.

It was gone.

Panic that rivaled being face to face with the Coiled Whale consumed him as he searched for his life support and only tie to the world familiar to him. He kicked his feet to propel him up over the surface of the sea to get a quick glimpse of his surroundings.

Nothing.

He pivoted and did this again and again, bursting out of the sea like a dolphin at play, only his maneuvers would have fatal consequence. After surveying the dark hills of the sea over and over, the thoughts of any beast attacking him had dissipated. His singular focus proved successful when a glint of moonlight shimmered in the distance. Again, it was the reflection off the metal band which held the barrel together that had saved his life.

He swam toward his only friend, held it in a long embrace, then secured his cloak to it once again. Before he knew it, sleep washed over him.

As the morning sun rose over the horizon, the heat went to work baking the moisture from the cloak. By the time Searlus awoke, the hood on his head felt like the disowned skin of a snake. It itched the back of his neck and felt so brittle that it would crack at the slightest irritation.

He had slept with his stomach on the barrel and hands in the water. The second sensation he felt upon waking, after the growing burn on his head and neck, was the numb swelling of his fingers. Where the hood of his cloak had become dry and cracking, his hands were waterlogged and bulging. He pulled them out of the water and held them in front of his face, one at a time, and was relieved to find they felt much larger than they were. Still, they tingled with the bulge of salt water.

After he'd addressed the hood and the hands, a third annoyance made itself known. On the ridge of his cheek, where the bone slopes down into the eye socket, he felt a small pricking. He knew a splinter when he felt it, for he had succumbed to more than he could count over the years in the shop. He reached his swelled sausage fingers up to his face and rubbed over the spot. There was a small barb on the otherwise smooth surface. When he attempted to pluck it free, he found his bulging fingers were too bloated for the task.

Time ticked on as he wrestled with the unwelcome guest. The longer the makeshift surgery went on, the more his frustrations rose. It was getting hotter and hotter as the sun reached high noon, he hadn't eaten in over a day, no water to quench his thirst, no sign of rescue, and he still couldn't get the cursed splinter from his cheek. He repeated his refrain in the loudest yell his parched throat could muster.

"Curse you!"

The pattern continued; yelling, cursing the Wavemaker, surveying his surroundings for life, picking the splinter, bobbing his head underwater to cool down, trying to sleep, yelling, cursing the Wavemaker.

Early afternoon melted into early evening. Searlus was still stuck in his pattern, except for the splinter. His fingers had returned to their normal size, and he was able to pluck what he hoped was the entire splinter from his face. There was a dull itch in the spot, which he didn't know if it was caused by the skin being irritated, or if the splinter had broken off under the skin.

It was during the last rotation of yelling curses before the sun went down that something changed. He was still soaked through and had almost no feeling in his feet. Exhaustion from the lack of sleep, food, and excessive heat had nearly overtaken him yet again. There was no visible sign of life in any direction. But he heard something far off behind him.

The voice of a man.

# 14

## ADRIFT

Searlus snapped his head in the direction of the sound and started swimming. There was no second guessing. No questioning. That single, faint human voice was the only flicker of hope he had. His pace was half of his normal speed, slowed both by fatigue and the barrel. He had tied the back of his cloak to the metal band as he ferried it across the sea. He didn't see a ship or land on the horizon, so he figured he would still need his life support.

He paddled along, hearing the voice sputter something every few moments. At the sound of each new utterance, Searlus shifted course and pointed his head toward the sound. Each yell grew louder. The sun had set and the stars dotted the sky. Sea wind carried the voice to him and he recognized the words for the first time.

"We sail on the surge of the raging sea, the ship the seed of the golden tree..."

It was the Holy Shanty. A warm wave of relief washed over him. He hated that a fellow Horak had been thrown overboard, but he was glad to not be swimming directly into a skirmish with a ruthless Zamarian. As he swam he wondered if he would be relieved even to see a Zamarian in these conditions.

There was no time for a conclusion to be made because the clearest line of the shanty rang out, and a ping of recognition flashed in Searlus' mind as he continued swimming. He recognized the voice. It wasn't Navas, he knew that for a fact. It was too old and tired. He'd never heard the High Captain sing the Holy Shanty, except for the first night, but that was with the whole group. The Wavemaker wouldn't let someone like the High Captain be thrown overboard anyway.

Captain Nimrad's voice was much too high to match this low, scratchy wail. Searlus knew he would soon confirm his suspicion as he was nearly upon the voice.

"Horah, friend," Searlus said out with his dry voice. A split second later, the old voice said with a boom.

"Horah!"

With that warm greeting, Searlus could see a dark figure floating in water just ahead of him. The moonlight bathed the sea with white, and the man swam in his direction. In that moment, the exhaustion seemed to have disappeared, his legs kicked at double time, and the broken splinter in his cheek stopped its stinging. This was no rescue, but it was something. He knew he could survive out here a little longer with a fellow Horak at his side.

The two had come face to face, and the old man was the first to recognize his fellow cast away.

"Ah, Searlus son of Dovar."

"Captain Hemol?"

"Aye," Captain Hemol said. Searlus could see the old man's frail silhouette clinging to a piece of jagged driftwood. "You look like the inside of a filleted tarpon. Get some sleep. I'll take the first watch."

"Last time I really slept was on the *Gildenglory*," Searlus said.

"Go on, then," Captain Hemol said. "We'll make a plan after we can't sleep anymore." A small grin grew on Searlus' face. The next moment he secured himself to his barrel and pulled his cloak over his head. He planned to thank the Wavemaker for this brief respite from the constant terror of the sea, but he passed out as soon as he shut his eyes.

Searlus woke with a start the next morning. With his body half submerged in the sea, he splashed about yelling "Save me! Save me!"

"Easy, boy," a coarse voice said. Searlus pulled his cloak from his head and the mid-morning sun blinded him. Instinctively he covered his eyes, and in that moment the reality of his hopeless situation came back to him. A bout of misplaced aggression bubbled up inside him.

"You let me sleep through the night," Searlus said, accusing Captain Hemol.

"You were quite tired, it seemed," Captain Hemol said.

"Who kept watch, then? There could have been a ship or something. The Coiled Whale could have returned."

"I did," Captain Hemol said. He was looking down,

carving something into his piece of driftwood with a small dagger.

"You must have slept?" Searlus asked.

"Slept straight through the night before. Was able to get my old self up on this plank. A bit stiff, but not much different than the cots in the *Gildenglory*." Captain Hemol laughed at his own joke. Searlus floated in silence. Captain Hemol kept carving.

"What now?" Searlus asked after a few moments of silence.

"I'm not sure," Captain Hemol said without looking up from his carving. "Tell me, do you render the 'us' in the holy texts as granular, down to the individual? Or do you use 'us' as synonymous with 'the family of Horaks?'"

"We're stranded at sea," Searlus said. He involuntarily punctuated the last word with a hint of anger. "The Sea of Beasts, to be specific."

"Well, yes," Captain Hemol said. He paused for a beat, then looked up to Searlus for the first time this morning. "Oh no. You're going mad."

"I'm not going mad," Searlus said to the old man. The sun caused deep shadows in the wrinkles of the old captain's face. His leathery skin reflected the sun. "I just want to get out of here, and all you want to do is arts and crafts."

"Very well," Captain Hemol said. He tucked the dagger into his cloak. "What shall we do?"

"I don't know. Swim somewhere. To an island or something?"

"Which way?"

"How should I know? You've sailed these seas."

"I've never seen an island in this sea," Captain Hemol said. "There must be some, of course, but we haven't mapped any. Which means—"

"They'd be uninhabited." Searlus finished the sentence as the grave realization sunk in.

"Precisely," Captain Hemol said.

"It's still our best chance," Searlus said, trying to sound confident.

"That makes sense," Captain Hemol said. "So, which way shall we swim?"

"You're not helping. You want to live, don't you?" Searlus asked.

"Oh, yes. It's been a good life, praise the Wavemaker."

"Then let's make a plan," Searlus said like he was talking to a small child.

"It's no use, really," Captain Hemol said, causing Searlus to do a double-take. "We could choose a direction, based on the position of the stars, and swim. We'd know which direction we're swimming, let's say south, but that's a little like jumping from the crow's nest and know you're going down.

"We could realistically swim for a few days, maybe. Catch a few fish. If we get lucky it will rain and we'll have some water. Five days pass. Chances are, we won't find an island. But there could be an island two days to the east. And we'd miss it. It's a gamble."

"We have to try something," Searlus said.

"Do we?" Captain Hemol asked. Searlus didn't have a rebuttal. The waves carried them up and down in near silence. Searlus stared into the tired gray eyes of his only friend. Then, Captain Hemol's face relaxed. He pulled the dagger from his cloak and started carving yet again. "Listen, son, best to conserve our energy and let the waves carry us where they will. The Wavemaker keeps his eye on the starfish. You know this, yes?"

"I've read the holy texts," Searlus said.

"Then he knows we're here, too," Captain Hemol said with certainty. "Now, how do you translate Letter 18?"

. . .

After the rocky start to the day, Searlus cooled off and let the currents carry him wherever the Wavemaker willed. The rest of the light hours passed quicker than the previous day. Captain Hemol kept the conversation going, asking how Searlus understood a certain section of the holy text, or asking Searlus about his father and mother. The highlight of the day for Searlus was when Captain Hemol talked about life in the Lightholm.

It was late in the day, and the oath Searlus had made while in the grasp of the Coiled Whale kept badgering him like an angry bee. He had trouble focusing on what Captain Hemol was saying, and the hopelessness of their situation began to rise in him again.

"The beatings do seem more random than when I was your age," Captain Hemol said, half reminiscing, half lamenting. "You're right about that."

"When is enough, enough?" Searlus said with an edge in his voice. "When do we fight back?"

"I trust you know how that worked out for the revolt in Salumoor."

"That was a hundred years ago," Searlus said.

"Only a fool would believe King Tiveros has forgotten."

"They're killing us. Can't pay the tariffs? Jailed. Forget to hail King Tiveros? Whack with the club. Say something a Saluman guard doesn't like? Whack, whack, dead."

"We must trust the Wavemaker, Searlus."

"We must fight back," Searlus said. "The Wavemaker has given us brains and strength. We outnumber the Salumans three to one. The Isles of Hor belong to us."

"I know this, child," Captain Hemol said in his characteristic cool, calm voice. "I remember running the streets of Tarsa as a boy. Down to the market, to the beach, up in the hills. All day, playing with my mates. We wouldn't see a single Saluman guard. We feared for nothing." Captain Hemol's voice trailed off. "I know."

"Then you know something must be done," Searlus pleaded.

"The Wavemaker is moving. Steady, Searlus. Steady."

"It doesn't matter," Searlus said. "We'll never see the shores of Ramooth of again."

"You take first watch," Captain Hemol said. The sun had only just begun its descent. Searlus figured there were a few hours of daylight left. But, in the next moment, Captain Hemol pulled himself up onto his plank, tucked his knees to his chest, and pulled his hood over his head.

Searlus spent the remaining daylight hours trying to

find a way up onto his barrel. He hopped up on the side, but it rolled him off into the water. Just when he got his balance, an unexpected wave would come and knock him off. All the while Captain Hemol remained on his plank like a turtle on a log.

Night fell on the vast ocean yet again. Searlus' stomach ached and growled. Part of him worried it would echo so loud in the sea that some type of predator would think it was the sound of a dying animal. He forced himself to laugh at this but made a note to spend more time trying to catch a fish tomorrow. He had casually tried that day but was unsuccessful. They didn't come to the surface, he knew, because it was too hot. If he was going to catch something to eat, he'd have to leave his safety barrel and plunge down as deep as he could go. He wasn't ready for that yet.

The dark void below him didn't help.

Pitch black darkness surrounded him. The stars provided the only light, taking over the responsibility for the sliver of moon. The only way he could tell where the sky ended and the sea began was the lack of stars in the sea. He floated with his head on his barrel, like a pillow, and spent a considerable amount of time looking up at the stars, studying the constellations. He had only brief training in navigation in the Lightholm, but he was able to work out that they seemed to be drifting to the northwest.

The great tree constellation, *The Oak of Morah*, did look incredibly like the lone seabird constellation, *Mighty Yonah*, which would mean they were floating due south. He would wake Captain Hemol soon and ask him.

Searlus turned back over and floated upright in the sea. He did his habitual sweep of the sea around him, looking for any signs of life. There were no ships or dark outlines of land mass. But something did catch his eye. A single star shown in the sea near the horizon.

It rolled with the sea. Searlus looked up to the sky to find which star was responsible, but no light shone brighter than the rest. When he looked back down at the reflection he screamed.

The light was getting closer.

"Captain Hemol!" Searlus said. The captain woke with a splash, falling off his plank and into the sea. A moment later he popped back up above the water. "What is it, boy?"

"Look!" Searlus pointed toward the light. "It can't be."

"It is," Captain Hemol said, his voice deep. "A cursed luneshark."

# 15

## LUNESHARK

"Hand me your knife," Searlus said. Captain Hemol laughed.

"I'm fond of you, boy. But, you won't be getting the only weapon we have." Searlus saw Captain Hemol reach into his cloak and pull out the small dagger. "Get up on my plank, they've got a poisonous bite."

"And leave you to die?"

"I make my own decisions," Captain Hemol said. "Besides, if one of us will be shark food, it'll be me. The Wavemaker is not done with you yet." With that nonchalant encouragement, Captain Hemol pushed the plank toward Searlus and grabbed the barrel from him. By this time, the glow of the luneshark circled the two castaways, taunting them as it swam effortlessly through the water. Each rotation brought the beast closer.

Searlus obeyed his elder and pulled himself up on the piece of driftwood. Captain Hemol had made mounting the driftwood look deceptively easy. When Searlus tried to get his balance, his considerable weight toppled the back end of the plank, causing it to capsize, sending him splashing into the water.

"Good plan, trying to scare it away," Captain Hemol said when Searlus resurfaced. There was a slight smirk on his face. Searlus mumbled something under his breath and found the plank for attempt number two. He approached it slower this time and was able to get up on his hands and knees to maintain his balance. "Stay quiet, now," Captain Hemol said. "These cursed things can see about as good as a stone wall. Stay quiet and above the water and you'll be fine."

"What about you?"

"Shh," Captain Hemol said. Even after swapping his barrel for a plank, falling into the water, and mounting again, somehow he knew the luneshark's exact location. Now that he was steady, he locked his eyes on the glowing beast, and could see the outline of its white dorsal fin cutting through the surface of the water.

The words of his oath came back to him again.

Saved by the Coiled Whale only to be ripped apart by a luneshark. For a moment, that thought distracted him. What a strange thing, to think that he was saved by the Coiled Whale. He began to question if that was what really happened. It was dark and he was scared. Not to mention that he was underwater and near death. The Coiled Whale doesn't save people. It's a wild animal.

"Argh!" Captain Hemol screamed above a splash of water. Searlus was pulled from his daydream and found the lunehark an arms-length away. Water foamed and glowed as the shark attacked. The white glow turned a crimson tint as Captain Hemol slashed the beast with malicious intent. In a flash, the beast rattled its head before diving deep into the abyss.

The glow of the luneshark was gone.

"You killed it," Searlus said.

"Barely got it a scratch. They're all show. You get them good one time, and they turn tail."

"But the blood?"

"I've lost a little of my speed in my old age," Captain Hemol said. His voice more raspy than usual. "Help me on that plank, will you?" Searlus slid off the driftwood and held it steady as Captain Hemol pulled himself up. Searlus saw a shimmering darkness on Captain Hemol's left thigh. The old man ripped a piece of his cloak and tied it around his leg, above the wound. Searlus held the wood steady.

"I'll take first watch," Captain Hemol said.

"No," Searlus said in a tone that sounded more insubordinate than he intended. "I mean, you need to rest."

"Wouldn't be good for me to sleep now."

"But the poison?"

"Saltwater should help offset the toxins."

"Will it be back?"

"They're cowards if you get them good," Captain Hemol said. "Only managed to cut the end of his top fin off, just a bit. Should spook him enough, though."

"Yeah," Searlus said, his mind still reeling at the events that had just transpired. He tied his cloak back to the barrel out of habit, and his mind replayed the events of the last hour. He'd come face to face with a luneshark but hid in safety like a child while his elder captain fought the beast off and managed to slice him with his dagger, but at the cost of getting his leg mauled. Searlus resolved to not stand back in safety from that point forward. His mind raced as a thousand different fictional scenarios filled his mind, and in all of them he was the hero.

Then he fell asleep.

. . .

Searlus woke the next morning before the sun had risen above the horizon. A morning fog hung over the water. Captain Hemol was passed out on his plank, and Searlus breathed a sigh of relief when he heard the old man snoring. Captain Hemol had tied the laces of his boots to Searlus' barrel and Searlus stared at the bloodied leg. A cool breeze brought a steady rise and fall of the sea. It was the first breath of cold air Searlus had felt the entire journey. He guessed that meant they were floating north.

Captain Hemol yelled. Searlus jumped and the old captain splashed into the water. A moment later he popped back up out of the sea and began squeezing the water from his beard. "How'd you sleep?"

"What was that?" Searlus asked, ignoring the old man's question.

"What?"

"You yelled."

"Huh," Captain Hemol said. He pulled himself back up onto his plank and began untying his shoelaces and the tourniquet before he spoke. The sun had begun to peek over the edge of the sea. "Had a sea dream."

"Oh," Searlus said. "About a luneshark, I'm guessing."

"Giant clam," Captain Hemol said. "It's always the giant clams. Not sure why." Searlus didn't know how to reply. He swallowed a laugh. Captain Hemol was looking at his wound. Searlus wasn't sure if the sea dream was so ridiculous, or if he was just delirious, but the laugh he swallowed gurgled its way back to the surface.

Searlus broke out in an uncontrolled laugher.

"Giant clams," Searlus said through tears. "I'm sorry."

"Get it out," Captain Hemol smiled. "It's ridiculous. I know. I'd tell you the rest, but I don't know if you could handle it."

"There's more?" Searlus said. "Please. Do tell."

"When I was first learning the trade, sailing around the islands with my friends, the sea dreams would scare the piss out of me."

"I bet there's a ship on their way right now after hearing your scream."

"That's not what I mean," Captain Hemol said. His voice got low and serious. "I mean, literally." Searlus looked into the old man's eyes, trying to follow. Then, it clicked. The laughter welled up inside of him again. He fell back into the water in a laughing fit. His stomach hurt from lack of food, and now excessive laughter. He floated in the water on his back as he tried to get ahold of himself.

Searlus was in a surprisingly jovial mood the rest of

the morning, despite the weather not clearing from the morning fog. The sky was a grey lamb's skin as the thick clouds hovered low just over the surface of the water. Captain Hemol shared more stories from sailing when he was a boy. They debated which holy text was most significant for the Horaks. Searlus claimed Wayfinder Moshah's *Letter 91* was most important because it gave them the Wavemaker's code. They wouldn't know how to live otherwise. Captain Hemol said Wayfinder Yesha's *Letter 53* because it was the prophecy of the coming Mistrider who would transform the whole world into Gildenwood.

They went back and forth all morning, until the topic of the Lightholm was brought up. Searlus asked Captain Hemol questions about living there and Captain Hemol answered them all. He continued cleaning out his bite wound between answers. Searlus finally got a good look at it and knew it was worse than the captain was letting on. The old man didn't show any signs of slowing down though. Anytime there was a lull in conversation, Captain Hemol muttered or hummed the tune of the holy shanty. His spirits were high, as always. His voice gentle, as always. So, Searlus figured the best thing to do was to help the old man keep his mind off the amount of blood he'd lost, so he kept asking questions.

"Do you think I could have a place in the Lightholm?"

"Do you love the Wavemaker?"

"Of course," Searlus said without thinking.

"Then, yes," Captain Hemol said with certainty. "You can learn the finer points of the code, the tradition, the way. That's easy. What we need are more Horaks fully devoted to the Wavemaker."

The doubt Searlus had left unattended regarding his unfulfilled oath nagged at him. He claimed full devotion to the Wavemaker with his words, but his thoughts revealed otherwise. A disgust grew in him and compounded. He hated that he doubted the Wavemaker, but he couldn't shake the real doubt that the Wavemaker would be true to the oath and deliver him to safety.

The shame was real. The doubt was real. And, in that moment, something else was real and caught him off guard.

The song of a seabird.

Searlus jumped up to full attention, craning his neck as high as he could to spot the source of the sound. Captain Hemol looked confused.

"A bird," Searlus said.

"Where?" Captain Hemol asked.

"Do you hear it?"

"Ah. Hearing was the first thing to go for me. Can't hardly hear anything except what I can touch."

"Can you swim?" Searlus asked.

"Following you," the old man said. He rotated on his plank so he was belly down and could paddle with his arms. Searlus heard a painful exhale as Captain Hemol put weight on the luneshark wound. No questions were asked and no hesitations made. Searlus mounted the barrel in a similar way and began to paddle and kick into the fog, toward the song. The old captain followed.

After a few strokes, it became painfully clear to Searlus that Captain Hemol could not keep up. Even if he had not been injured, the old man would never have been able to keep pace with a man nearly forty years his junior. Searlus was an excellent swimmer and had spent most of his boyhood days at the beach. He tried to slow his pace in a way that wasn't obvious, so Captain Hemol could keep up. Searlus didn't mind going slower, as long as the birdsong continued to guide them.

"I'm old but I'm not stupid," Captain Hemol said during one of their breaks.

"I didn't—"

"You're sandbagging. I'm slowing you down."

"It's fine."

"Night's falling, and that means the sea birds will tuck in, too. Best to go on without me."

"If I find something, I'll come back to get you," Searlus said, weighing his options.

"Well yeah," Captain Hemol said in jest. "I thought that was assumed."

"I can't do it," Searlus said. "Can't leave you here."

Captain Hemol mumbled, looking over Searlus' shoulder. He pointed into the fog. "Looks like you don't have to."

Searlus spun around in the water and saw a dark column of cloud, a black sheep in the herd, rising high into the sky. He followed the smoke down toward the horizon, down toward the outline of a mountain silhouetted by the fog.

# 16

## LAND

Nothing more was said. They got belly down in the sea and kept swimming toward the land. Searlus made sure Captain Hemol was always close by, but it seemed the island gave the old captain a boost of energy. Sometime after nightfall, Searlus' barrel drifted into the sand. He slid off the barrel and felt his body sink into soggy earth. It was the first time he'd touched solid ground in a month. He waded out into the shallows and pulled Captain Hemol in. Once on the shore, they both collapsed on the sand.

"Feels like the sand is moving," Searlus said, exhausted.

"Praise the Wavemaker," Captain Hemol said.

"We need food," Searlus said. "And to find out where that smoke came from."

"The Wavemaker has heard our cries and answered our pleas. We must not forget the history of the Wavemaker's blessing."

"Yes," Searlus said, a hint of frustration growing in

his voice. "We're not safe here. There's someone else on this island and I want to find them before they find us." Captain Hemol began his muttering of the holy shanty and other fragments from the holy text. "I'll be right back."

Searlus pulled himself up from the sand. His sea legs wobbled from the weeks on the ship and the days submerged in the ocean. He took his first land step and fell to his knees. The soft sand cushioned his fall. Pushing himself back up into a stand, he was able to take a few hobbling steps toward a rock, which he used to brace himself. After a few moments of remembering how to walk, he felt comfortable enough to set off for the source of the smoke. Before he knew it, he was crouching and weaving his way through a dark jungle.

Leaves spooked him as they brushed the top of his head. He tried to move with as much grace and stealth as he could muster but traveling in an unknown forest by only the light of a foggy moon made his footfalls sound like rockslides. He felt his elevation changing into an ascent, and to his relief, he came to an opening that overlooked the source of the smoke. A huge bonfire was burning on another beach, and men sat around it drinking. A few tents were pitched to one side. Searlus noticed another group of men huddled in a tight group. His eyes drifted to a ship floating out at sea, and he froze in place when he saw the flag flying from the main mast.

The black and white flag of the Zamarians.

He backed away from the bluff and hid in the darkness. Just as he was turning to go back down the hill and share the news with Captain Hemol, he heard a voice that simultaneously brought a smile to his face and made his heart sink.

"Get your hands off of me, you dirty fox."

Navas.

Searlus peered back over the edge of the hill and spotted his friend below. A Zamarian sailor slapped him in the face, and Navas just stood there and took it. That's when Searlus realized his friend was bound in ropes, and the people he was bound to were fellow members of the *Gildenglory*. Searlus' first instinct was to run down to free his friend. He took a step before his rational mind caught up.

"I'll be back, friend," Searlus whispered to himself. He shuffled back down the hill toward the beach. Any hint of weak knees had vanished. He ran with the same speed and agility as when he was a boy running through the market with Navas. The only difference was now he dodged tree trunks instead of adults and ducked under canopies of leaves instead of linen. That running was for leisure. This was a rescue mission.

Captain Hemol lay in the same place as when Searlus left. The dark waves foamed up on the beach, just out of reach of the old man, before receding back into the ocean. He startled when Searlus came running out of the tree line.

"About scared me to death, boy," Captain Hemol said with a sigh.

"Navas," was all Searlus could say. His breath was labored.

"You see his ghost or something? What are you running from?"

"Zamarians," Searlus said, trying to get his breathing under control. "The smoke is from the Zamarians. They've set up camp on the other side of the island and they've got Horak prisoners." Captain Hemol breathed in a deep breath, held it a moment, and then let it out in a long, steady exhale.

"Wavemaker, help us," he mumbled before getting up to his feet. He stumbled on his bad leg, and Searlus caught him just before he fell over. "Thank you," he said. "Now, get me a stick or something."

Searlus left the old man balancing on the sand and ventured out into the shallow woods. He yanked at what he thought were a few downed branches, low and brushing the ground, but found them all still connected to their trees. He kept searching until, to his surprise, he pulled one free. He stuck the thickest end into the ground and the knotted branch spiraled up until the thinnest part, which he figured he could have dipped in ink and used as a quill, rose just above his head.

It was exactly what he needed.

There was no delay once Searlus gave the walking stick to Captain Hemol. Moments after pulling the stick from obscurity, they were making their slow trek up the hill. Searlus led the way through the dark forest. Captain Hemol hobbled behind. After twice the time it took Searlus to make the original hike, they finally reached the opening on the edge of the hill.

"We've got to rescue them," Searlus said before Captain Hemol could even catch his breath. "My friend is down there."

"Then what?" Captain Hemol said.

"Attack the Zamarians."

"With what weapons?"

"We can't do nothing," Searlus said louder than he intended.

"That's not what I'm saying," Captain Hemol said in his cool, calm voice. "They're not expecting us, so we've got that. They've got more men, and I'd bet my good leg they all have at least two blades each."

"Let's free our men, first, then we can retreat into the forest to regroup," Searlus said.

"Not a bad plan," Captain Hemol said. "But the best-case scenario is the Zamarians cut their losses, board their ship, and leave us stranded. Do you want to stay here?"

"You want to steal the Zamarian ship?" Searlus asked. "The High Captain would have our heads if he knew we set foot on that despicable vessel."

"The High Captain sees black and white when he looks through his spyglass," Captain Hemol said.

"Don't you always say we have to trust the Wavemaker? If we stay, he'll provide another way off the island."

"You're asking the Wavemaker to work two miracles," Captain Hemol said without skipping a beat. "Keep your eyes open and you'll see how he's already provided. I'm not dying on this island."

Searlus weighed the accusation in his mind. The thought of sailing on a Zamarian ship made him sick to his stomach. In his mind, it barely outweighed the alternative, which was being stranded on the island. But before he'd even have the chance to be disgusted, they would have to overpower the Zamarians.

"The Zamarians are mistreated and misunderstood," Captain Hemol continued. "Some are worse than others. Looks a rough lot down there, though."

"What's your plan, then?" Searlus asked.

"We need to rest, eat, and regain some strength before we try anything," Captain Hemol said in a way Searlus did not expect. "We'll stay hidden tomorrow, eating and observing the Zamarians. Tomorrow night we attack."

Searlus did not reply. He wanted to act now. Captain Hemol's raspy voice filled the silence.

"We'll keep an eye on your friend."

"Yeah," Searlus said. He laid down in the grass and kept his eyes on the prisoners. He heard Captain Hemol bedding down and muttering to himself. After a short time, the muttering faded into a light snore. Searlus kept watch on the group. Most of the Zamarians were drinking around the large fire. After a while, Searlus' eyelids grew heavy. He was about to doze off when a few Zamarians came off the ship shouting orders. The next moment a few of the men around the fire stood up wobbling. They tore down the tents around them and started for the ship. Searlus jumped when he realized what was happening.

The Zamarians were preparing to leave the island.

# 17

## RESCUE

Searlus rushed over to Captain Hemol and shook him awake.

"They're leaving. We have to go."

"What?" Captain Hemol said in a groggy growl.

"We can't wait until tomorrow night. We can't wait until tomorrow morning." Searlus paused, took a deep breath, and surveyed the scene unfolding below them. "I'm going now."

"Here," Captain Hemol said as Searlus took his first step. "I won't be much help, so I'll stay back. Get our boys free." With that command, Searlus saw the old man holding out the short blade that had once slit the fin of a luneshark. Searlus accepted the gift, tested the weight in his hand, and then set off down the hill toward the fire.

He crept at an even slower pace than if he'd been traveling with a crippled old man. The terrain was an uneven jungle of darkness. He tested his weight on every step. The tension of wanting to get to the beach before the Zamarians set sail conflicted with his innate desire for self-preservation and not wanting to hurt himself from a careless misstep. After what felt longer than the night he had just spent stranded in the ocean, the ground leveled out and he felt the soft give of sand beneath his feet.

The area which could have been mistaken for a lively festival when he first investigated the fire now looked like an abandoned ghost town. Shadows dotted the beach where holes in the sand had formed from Zamarian footsteps. The small holes led to larger holes, and Searlus wondered if they were burying something here. A pile of orange coals burned where the bonfire had raged. The prisoners stood bound together near the tree line, but the Zamarian guards were nowhere to be found. Searlus assumed they had loaded up on the boat, and they were going to leave the prisoners here, or the prisoners would be the last to be taken on board.

Stumbling out of the forest was a shadow heading straight for Searlus. With nowhere to hide, Searlus lunged toward the man. As he approached, he could see the unkempt beard and long knotted hair of the lone Zamarian guard. Searlus closed the gap between them in a hurry and with a flash of steel impaled the guard before he could sound the alarm. The man gasped as the air escaped his pierced lungs and blood littered the sand.

As the man fell to the ground, his dead weight ripped the blade from Searlus' hand. He hurried over to the man to retrieve Captain Hemol's dagger before freeing his friends. The man stared up at Searlus with red-rimmed, glassy, bloodshot eyes. He gasped one last airy breath.

"Wavemaker, have mercy."

Searlus was gone before the man closed his eyes for the last time. He ran on the edge of the beach toward the prisoners. His eyes darted around the edge of the forest for any other Zamarian wanderers. He found no other living being. Only his friends, who were coming within an arm's length.

"I told you to back off, you dirty fox," Navas said from the darkness.

"Quiet, you fool," Searlus said. "It's me, Searlus." The group of prisoners fell silent. "Hold still." The Horak men all stood impossibly still as Searlus approached. He began sawing at the ropes binding his friend's hands.

"How?" Navas asked.

"The Wavemaker works in mysterious ways," Searlus said.

"You died. You were thrown overboard," Navas said in a dream-like voice.

"Let's catch up later," Searlus said. "I just killed one of their guards. There's probably more." Searlus took a deep breath. "You boys ready to show them what full-blooded Horaks are made of?"

Silence.

"Hey!" a slurred voice shouted behind him.

Searlus pulled his dagger from the sliced rope and pointed it toward the voice. A bead of sweat ran down the side of his face and was lost in his beard. He adjusted his grip on the dagger, squeezing it tight. It was time for some holy vengeance.

"Any of yous dung beetles seen the captain?" the voice bobbled up and down. "He told me I could drive the ship if only I kept a good eye on the Horak scum."

"Aye," a voice called out from the ground. It was then that Searlus realized the dark shadows in the sand were not shadows at all. The whole Zamarian crew had passed out drunk on the beach, and he had walked right through them completely unaware. "I said no such thing," the voice continued.

"Aye!" the Zamarian sailor said. He turned toward the voice of the captain but as soon as he took the first step, he forgot to lift his foot and he collapsed with a muted thud into the sand.

"Let's go," Searlus said under his breath. By this time Navas had helped the other Horaks loose the ropes from their hands and feet, and the last of the prisoners were getting free.

"Hide in the jungle," Navas whispered.

"No," Searlus said louder than he intended. A shadow shuffled nearby. "To the ship."

"Have you lost your mind?"

"I don't like it either."

"The Wavemaker will strike us down the moment we set sail," Navas said.

"I've got a friend here who thinks otherwise," Searlus said. "Trust me." Navas stared at his friend for a moment.

The Zamarian shadow shuffled again, only this time he didn't settle. It took him a moment to get to his feet. He stumbled past the other shadows, past the smoldering embers, towards the sea. His feet sank in the wet sand

and the water foamed around his ankles. He rubbed his eyes and surveyed the entire length of the beach before screaming at the top of his lungs.

Searlus watched the whole scene unfold from the front of a small boat on its way to the Zamarian ship.

# 18

## THE CAPTAIN

When Searlus led the Horak escapees toward the ship, they crammed as many men as they could into the two small boats the Zamarians were using to get from the ship to the shore. The handful of men who couldn't fit on the boats decided to swim toward the ship, rather than waiting for the small boat to return. Searlus was the first aboard the Zamarian ship, and he crept around the deck with his dagger at the ready. He found one man standing at the helm, with a long staff in his hand. It appeared he had watched them approach.

"I almost left without you," an airy voice said from the darkness. Searlus recognized the old man's voice immediately.

"How'd you get here?" Searlus said as he lowered the dagger.

"There were three boats on the shore. Didn't want you to have to come back for me if the Zamarians all woke up," Captain Hemol said. "You were coming back for me, right?"

"Of course," Searlus said. "Glad I don't have to, though."

"Captain Hemol?" Navas asked.

"In the flesh," the old captain said. "Got marooned with your buddy here. Looks like things are working out, though." More Zamarian yells echoed through the darkness. Water splashing complemented the yells. "Best to catch up later," Captain Hemol said in a playful tone.

"Get to your places," Searlus said to the crew surrounding him. "Drop the main sail and get us out of here." In an instant the Horak crew got to work readying the ship for their swift departure. Searlus kept an eye on the incoming Zamarians as they swam toward the ship. Any trace of worry faded from him as the main sail dropped and was secured in place. It filled with wind and in the next moment the ship cut through the water, leaving the island and the Zamarians in their wake. The island, along with the screams, faded into the darkness.

The open sea graced them with relatively smooth sailing. Once Searlus was confident they were far out of the reach of the Zamarians, he gave the order to raise the main sail, which brought them to a near standstill in the water.

"Come together," he said. The men finished their jobs and gathered around the main mast. Searlus surveyed the men, silently counting all those aboard. "Sixteen," he said after a moment.

"That's not even half a crew," Navas said. "We can't

sail a rig like this with sixteen men." The men began to grumble to each other.

"Wait," Searlus said above the noise. "Before we make any decisions, or share any doubts, this ship needs a captain. And I nominate Captain Hemol." The whole crew turned toward the old man, who stood leaning on his makeshift cane.

"Ha, I'm much too old to captain a ship."

"By the code of the Lightholm, the eldest certified captain takes control of a vessel if there is a vacancy."

"I'm also injured," Captain Hemol said. Then, he said something that sent the men on the ship back into their hushed mumbles. "I nominate Searlus of Ramooth to be captain of this vessel."

Searlus stood in shock. He hadn't completed his training in the Lightholm and was one of the youngest among them. The murmurs grew louder until a squeaky voice spoke from the pack of Horaks.

"Oh, yeah!" a young man said. "I vote for Searlus, too." Searlus turned and felt a bit of joy in his chest when he saw the voice belonged to the young Horak he met in the Lightholm as their journey began.

"Shut up, Jok," a man with a deep growl said. Kaius was the only Horak who incited the same anger in Searlus as the Salumans. The teenage Horak furled his brows and stepped out of the circle. Kaius continued. "I nominate Captain Zadoah. He's second eldest."

All eyes swung to Captain Zadoah as he stood apart from the group, leaning against a barrel. He was just as frail as Captain Hemol, if not more so. His tangled white beard hung down to his chest.

"No, no, no," he said under his breath.

"I'll do it," Captain Hemol said in an instant. He strode up next to Searlus and addressed the group. "By order of the Lightholm of the Holy Wavemaker, I accept responsibility of this vessel and every soul which shall step foot aboard her decks."

"Let it be so," Searlus said. The men mumbled the same words in unison.

"Alright, Captain, what now?" Searlus asked.

"My first order as Captain is to resign my captaincy and appoint Searlus of Ramooth as captain of this vessel, by order of the Lightholm of the Holy Wavemaker."

Silence fell over the deck. The men stood dumbfounded at the events which had just unfolded. Kaius stood with his jaw clenched.

"Let it be so," an old voice said from the main mast. Captain Zadoah confirmed it. The Horak crew had no choice but to affirm the decision.

"Let it be so," the men repeated.

"Uh, we've got another problem," someone said from the door going below deck. The entire crew turned and saw Jok standing on the top stair with two women wearing long, thin linen dresses.

The entire crew roared. Some men were calling it an outrage. Others a blessing from the Wavemaker. Amidst the commotion, Searlus called for Jok to take the women below deck and asked Captain Hemol and Navas to join.

. . .

"Did you kill the Zamarians then?" one of the

women asked as she plopped down onto a chipped wooden chair. Jok had taken them into the first room off the stairs. It was one of the few rooms with a door.

"No," Searlus said. "Not all of them."

"Wish you would've," the other woman added. She sat gingerly on the hammock near the wall.

"What are your names, ladies?" Captain Hemol asked.

"Manners?" The woman on the chair said. "Sis, they've got manners. You're gonna like this crew."

"I'm Thea," the woman by the wall said as she began a gentle swing on the hammock. "Please excuse my sister Cora. Wish I could say it was being the Zamarian slaves that made her like this, but she was born with her mouth running."

"Life's too short," Cora said. She got up and made her way toward a wooden trunk near the door. She pulled open the lid.

"You're Salumans," Searlus said.

"Nothing gets past this one," Cora said, rummaging through the linens.

"We've lived in Salumoor our whole life," Thea began. "Some friends wanted to sail down The Great River and touch Our Protection—"

"That gaudy giant eagle statue," Cora said over her sister.

"Yes, Our Protection," Thea continued. Cora didn't look up from the trunk. "Young people do it all the time after completing the academy."

"And just our luck, a storm rolls in and spits us right

out into the channel, turns our small boat over, but the nasty crew of this ship saved us from the sea."

"Our friends weren't so lucky," Thea looked down as she spoke.

"I'm sorry to hear that," Captain Hemol said. "May the Wavemaker have mercy."

"Wavemaker?" Cora said, looking up. "Oh, right. Your sky king."

"Excuse my sister," Thea said.

"How long have you been prisoners?"

"Not sure. Months."

"That's horrible," Navas spoke for the first time.

"He speaks!" Cora said. "There it is." She held a small pistol in the air with a grin on her face. Searlus and Navas went stiff.

"Put that down," Navas said. He pulled a sword from his side. Cora laughed.

"What? This?" Cora said, pointing the gun at Captain Hemol. He only smiled.

"Oh, I'm not the captain. That would be Searlus."

"Aren't you a little young to be a captain?" Cora said, turning the gun on him.

"I didn't want it," Searlus said.

"Oh, back off, Cora. You're not going to shoot anybody."

"Give me the gun," Navas said.

"You'll have to kill me, first. What will your Wavemaker think of that?"

"Let her keep it," Captain Hemol said.

"It's my gun," Cora yelled. "I hid it from those Zamarian asses before they locked us up."

"She's not wrong," Thea said.

"Fine, keep it. Yes." Searlus said, trying to cut the tension. "We need to figure out what to do with you."

"How about a hot meal to start?" Thea asked.

. . .

After his discussion with the prisoners, Searlus' first order as captain was to take down the black and white Zamarian flag from high upon the main mast. Someone tied a brick to it and threw it overboard. He dismissed any questions about the prisoners and ordered everyone to get some rest. The two sisters slept in the same room where they'd been interrogated and Searlus kept the night watch while the men wandered around below deck, trying to find somewhere to sleep. He did a round below deck as everyone was getting settled and found the ship in worse shape than he would have guessed.

The hall was littered with doors broken off their hinges, foodstuffs scattered on the floor of the mess hall all the way to the sleeping quarters. Most bunks had been pulled from the walls. Blankets and other personal belongings of the Zamarians were piled in corners of rooms. But that wasn't the worst of it. There was a rotten odor that seemed to be seeping out of the hull. Searlus' best guess was that the Zamarians had caught some tarpon and filleted them right here in the hallway, then left the scales and guts to decompose. He finished his round and headed back up to the deck.

Searlus sat on a crate on the bow of the ship. The water was as still as the air. The roar of the men below deck had died down, leaving Searlus alone with the sea. He had hardly had time to process the events of the last few days and couldn't believe that just four days ago he was sailing comfortably on the *Gildenglory* with a full crew and a full stomach.

Now, he questioned if he'd ever see those men again.

He questioned if he'd ever see anyone again.

The oath he'd made surfaced in his mind. He debated and rationalized yet again if the Wavemaker had fulfilled the oath. He was still stranded at sea, only this time his life support was a ship, not a barrel, and his company was a half-crew of escaped prisoners, not an elderly man. The fact remained.

"This doesn't count as rescue," Searlus said aloud.

"It's better than being a Zamarian slave," a voice said from behind him. Searlus turned and found Navas approaching.

"What are we going to do?" Searlus asked.

"You're the captain, now."

"I'm not qualified."

"That doesn't mean you don't want it." Searlus was silent. Every Horak boy dreamed of being the captain of a massive ship. Searlus didn't think it would happen until after he'd completed his training in the Lightholm, and he never dreamed it would be behind the wheel of a Zamarian ship. "We've got to turn back, right?" Navas said, breaking the silence.

"To the Lightholm?"

"Where else?" Navas asked.

"Gildenwood," Searlus said. "We're close. We've got to be close."

"You're serious? We don't know how to get there."

"Captain Hemol does."

"We've got Saluman women on board."

"We're this close."

"We can't get in."

"We could meet the *Gildenglory* there."

"What if we're too late?"

"Then we turn around and come home," Searlus said. "Don't you want to see it? The High Captain only selects a few members of the crew to go in anyway. We wouldn't see inside. We've still got to see it, though. We might never get this chance again."

"The crew won't like it," Navas said. "Especially after being plucked out of the sea only to be made Zamarian prisoners. They've been through too much."

"Heading home is just as dangerous. More storms. More Zamarian ships. If we sail toward Gildenwood, it gives them something to hope for." Navas was silent for a while. The boat continued to drift in the water. The first light of day began to fill the sky as they spoke, even before the sun broke the horizon. After a long while, Navas turned to his friend and placed his hand on Searlus' shoulder.

"At your service, Captain." He gave his friend a nod then headed off across the deck. Searlus dropped his face into his hands and mumbled a prayer.

"Fill our sails, Sacred Gail. Lead us to Gildenwood, then home to the shores of the Isles of Hor, and I'm your servant until I take my last breath."

# 19

## THE CREW

A collective groan like the song of a whale filled the ship when Searlus announced the plan to sail north toward Gildenwood. There were no objections, though. Navas and Captain Hemol vocalized their support, and within the first hour after sunrise, the sails had been dropped and the bowsprit pointed due north.

Searlus asked Captain Hemol to join him in the captain's quarters. The two men entered through double-doors. Searlus had been the only Horak to enter the captain's room, and he hadn't spoken a word of what he'd found. Now, Captain Hemol laughed as he entered.

"Tell me you cleaned this already?" he said with a chuckle.

"I haven't touched a thing."

Captain Hemol broke out in a raspy fit. The wood plank floor was spotless and looked recently polished. A deep, mahogany desk with intricate carvings up and down the sides and front sat anchored to the floor. The top of the desk was clear of any junk. Another table had been pushed against the opposite wall, with chairs neatly arranged. The air in the cabin smelled like the forest they had just escaped. Two plants with their green leaves overflowing hung from windows on both sides of the cabin. The bed in the far corner had neatly folded linen resting on top, with all creases patted out. When Captain Hemol's eyes landed on the bed, he broke out laughing again.

"Guess they're not so different than us," Captain Hemol said. He walked over to a plant suspended in the air. He took out his dagger and cut the thin rope holding it up. The pot crashed to the ground, soil and plant spilling everywhere.

"Hey!" Searlus said louder than he intended.

"You don't want the men to see this," Captain Hemol said. He strode over to a cabinet filled with porcelain trinkets and cups. He used the butt of the knife to break the glass, then pulled out a few teacups and tossed them across the room. Small sharp fragments of white littered the dark wood floor.

"That's enough," Searlus said.

"You've been below deck, yes?"

"Yes," Searlus said, not hiding his disgust.

"You've got to earn their trust. Give them no reason to hate you. Even a pinhole in the hull of a ship will sink it given enough time."

Searlus looked around the room. His eyes landed on a painting of a Coiled Whale attacking a ship. He pulled it from the wall and split the canvas over his knee, then tossed it in the corner.

"Too far," Captain Hemol said in mock outrage. Searlus looked at him with palms upturned. "I'm kidding." Captain Hemol said. "Well, kind of. That was a rare piece by the late Horak artist Zahlel. But some things are more important than art. It's a short list, but people are up there. Shame though."

"Sorry," Searlus said.

"No, no, no," Captain Hemol hushed him. "This why you brought me here?"

"Not at all," Searlus said. "You know how to get to Gildenwood, right?"

"You already made the plan to sail to Gildenwood," Captain Hemol. "And you don't know how to get there?"

"I thought you did."

"I do," Captain Hemol said. He smiled. "Looks like you've got faith yet, boy."

"So, you'll be my Wayfinder?"

"Whatever you need, Captain." Searlus' shoulders dropped, like the plant Captain Hemol had cut down earlier. He felt a little better about his plan. "You need some rest. The waters which lead to Gildenwood are not easy."

"Thank you, Wayfinder Hemol." Searlus made his way to the bed in the corner and began pulling the blankets back.

"What are you doing?" Wayfinder Hemol asked.

"You said I needed rest."

"Oh, you can't sleep in here," Wayfinder Hemol said. "You'll have a mutiny before your head hits the pillow."

"But we destroyed it all?" Searlus asked.

"Just needed to blow off some steam. Felt good, huh?"

"I guess," Searlus said.

"I'm feeling pretty good," Wayfinder Hemol said. "You need to address the crew regarding our guests. Make sure these boys behave. But first, find an empty hammock below deck and get a couple hours of shut eye. Should be quiet. I'll make sure the men are in line, and that they know you're sleeping among them."

"Thanks," Searlus said. He had day-dreamed about sleeping in the big, comfortable bed with actual blankets from the moment he first saw it the night before. But he trusted Wayfinder Hemol and knew there would be plenty of difficulties ahead, and he'd be better off not adding to them. He figured a dry, smelly hammock was better than a soggy barrel in the ocean every time.

He was wrong.

When Searlus stumbled back onto the deck after a short rest, his neck ached and his left hand tingled. The sun shone bright, but the air was cooler than he expected. Dark clouds filled the skyline due north of their current position, in the direction they were sailing.

"Captain on deck," he heard a voice shout. Navas joined his friend after making the announcement.

"Still not used to that," Searlus said.

"You will," Navas said.

"How are the men? They need to eat. Should we stop to fish? Do we need a break?"

"They're fine," Navas said. "Better than fine, really. The Zamarians have some bread and fish salted below deck. It's not your mom's cooking, but better than the leaves they fed us on the island."

"I can't tell if that's an insult or a compliment," Searlus said.

"Good," Navas said. "One of the men found the stash of rum, too. That boosted morale last night."

"No one will say it, but Zamarian rum is the best," Searlus said.

"I can't disagree with the captain."

"So, things are okay?" Searlus asked.

"Well," Navas said, pausing before continuing. "Cora and Thea decided they didn't like being locked up in their room."

"Wayfinder Hemol told me I need to address the crew to keep the women safe."

"I don't think that'll be a problem," Navas said. He pointed across the deck and saw Cora and Kaius having a drinking contest with most of the crew in a half circle around them.

"Kaius looks like he's seen Hakov's ghost," Searlus said.

"I think they can hold their own. Said they'd help with the mending of the cloaks if the men don't act like fools. The crew straightened right up after that," Navas said. "That's the least of our problems, though."

He pointed toward the dark clouds ahead of them.

"Of course," Searlus said. "It's too soon. We can't put them through another storm. Let's drop sails and hope it passes."

"I'll make the announcement," Navas said.

"Let me do it." Navas nodded and Searlus made his way to the helm. He heard Navas gathering the men. Searlus stood just above them and froze as he looked into the eyes of his crew. The furled brows from the day before had been smoothed out. Jaws were sharp and defined as men stood clinching them. A few men swayed back and forth with unease.

"Crew of the *Oathslaker*," Searlus called out. "I trust you have found some R&R, by which I mean rest and rum." Some of the men cheered. Searlus smiled. "I'm glad to hear it. There's no hiding what lies ahead. Those clouds look nasty, and I want nothing to do with them. We're going to raise the sails and wait it out. Wavemaker willing, it will pass by us to the east and we can continue north."

"What if it doesn't?" a voice called from the crowd of men. Searlus turned toward the voice and recognized Kaius waiting expectantly for an answer. The usual scowl had disappeared from his face and he looked like he'd just lost his mother in the market.

"Then we sail on," Searlus said with as much courage as he could muster. "We ready the ship for the worst but hope for the best." There was a long silence after these words. Searlus had meant them to inspire but now he feared they sounded ominous.

"Ready the ship for the storm, but pray she passes us by. May the Wavemaker guide us."

"Horah!" Navas yelled from among the men. The rest of the men repeated the chant twice more before Navas started shouting orders. Searlus watched as the crew scattered. Some began taking anything not nailed down below deck. Others began lowering the main sails. Wayfinder Hemol joined Searlus on the helm.

"*Oathslaker*, huh?" Wayfinder Hemol asked. "I think there's more to you than you're letting on."

"I'll tell you everything when we reach the Isles of Hor," Searlus said.

"I hope we get the chance," Wayfinder Hemol said looking to the dark clouds. "That storm is not going to miss us."

"What happened to having faith?" Searlus asked.

"Oh, I believe the Wavemaker can guide us through it. But I also know how to read the wind."

"Should I gather the crew back?"

"No, no," Wayfinder Hemol said. "They already know, too. Was good for them to see you're not just looking for a thrill. Some of them might think you actually care about them."

"I do care about them," Searlus said.

"Matters little if they don't believe you though, does it?"

"I'm trying," Searlus said.

"Not going to happen overnight. Get them through this storm, and you'll have their trust soon."

"I'm scared," Searlus said in a near whisper.

"Me too, boy," Wayfinder Hemol said. "That's another thing you've got in common with these men. Use it."

Searlus nodded and Wayfinder Hemol patted him on the back before making his way down the stairs to the main deck. He still hobbled with the branch Searlus had given him on the island. Searlus stood on the helm for a few moments, gathering his thoughts. The deck began to dip and rise with greater intensity. He looked over the side of the ship and his fears were confirmed. The waters were already growing rough.

"Will you keep your end of the oath, even still?" Searlus asked.

He took a deep breath and made his way below deck to make himself useful. He helped carry some barrels from the deck to a storage room. A handful of harpoons were scattered on the floor of the armory, so he placed them back on their wall hooks. Everyone who saw him helping gave him a nod as he passed.

After a few hours of cleaning the deck and making it scarce of any loose objects, Searlus found himself gathering extra rope to use during the storm. The youngest crew member, Jok, was in the dank, moldy room with him. They were winding the loose ropes up in nice, coiled piles.

"You've lived in Tarsa your whole life, then?" Searlus asked. Jok laughed.

"That'd be nice. Mom dragged me to every island in the bay. Except Hevraun, of course."

"Moving that many times in fifteen years," Searlus said. "Must've been rough."

"I'm sixteen," Jok said with his chest puffed out. He was still untying the tangled rope. "Had my birthday while we were tied up by the Zamarians."

"Well, Happy Birthday," Searlus said. "Once we get through this storm, we'll have a proper celebration.

Whole crew. We'll catch some fresh tarpon and cook it up special."

"You mean it?"

"Am I the captain of this vessel?" Searlus asked with mock authority.

"Kind of," Jok said, smiling.

"At least someone on this ship is honest," Searlus said with a laugh. Just then, the ship lurched backwards causing both Searlus and Jok to fall onto the moldy wooden floor. "Let's take these up to the deck." The two men grabbed a handful of the freshly coiled rope and made their way to the surface. Searlus offered to take some of the rope from Jok, who had it piled in his arms up over his head, but Jok refused.

"I can see," he said every time Searlus asked to bear some of the weight.

The first thing Searlus noticed when they reached the deck was how dark it had grown. It was early evening and the dark clouds were closing in, blocking the sunset. The waves had doubled in size since Searlus had gone below deck a few hours before. The ship lurched again, and Jok stumbled and dropped his ropes.

"Easy," Searlus said to the boy. "Just leave them. I'll come back and get them."

"I can do it," Jok said.

Searlus made his way toward the foremast and began securing the extra rope to the hook nearby in case a line snapped during the storm. Jok did the same thing on the side of the foremast between the mast and the front rail of the ship. Searlus finished securing his rope and looked straight ahead at Jok balancing the coiled rope, searching the pile for the frayed end.

Then, in an instant, the ship took a nose-dive into a particularly deep trough causing a wave of water to wash over the bow. Searlus grabbed hold of the mast and held on tight. The wave passed in a blink. Searlus washed the salt water from his eyes and looked ahead.

Jok was gone.

# 20

## THE TEST

"No!" Searlus yelled. A few of the nearby crew members rushed to Searlus' side and pulled him away from the edge of the ship, back toward the main mast in the middle of the deck. Searlus collapsed to his knees with his face in his hands.

"Take him to the captain's quarters," Searlus heard an old voice say. The two men who had pulled him from the edge of the ship helped him to his feet and led him to the room just off the main deck. "Lay down," Wayfinder Hemol said, pointing to the bed. Searlus obeyed.

"He was just there," Searlus said. "We just brought up the ropes. Birthday tonight. He's here." Wayfinder Hemol dismissed the men. Searlus felt his body rise and fall as the ship sailed into the unsteady waves. He closed his eyes and saw Jok standing on the bow securing the extra rope. The ship hit another swell and Searlus' eyes flashed open. Jok was gone. Just as fast as it had happened on the deck.

"I've already ordered the men to raise the sails,"

Wayfinder Hemol said as he pulled up a chair near the bed. "We're looking for him."

"We'll find him," Searlus said.

"Perhaps," Wayfinder Hemol said. "The sea is a merciless companion. We need her for food, to reach Gildenwood. But she is not kind to the desires of men."

"We'll find him," Searlus said again.

"Get some rest," Wayfinder Hemol said. "I'll wake you when we find him." The next moment, Searlus was alone. He stared up at the wood above the bed. A sun, moon, and stars had been carved into the dark oak. Searlus counted the stars until he fell asleep.

He woke a short time later.

The cabin was empty. By the sway of the ship, he knew the storm was upon them. He tried to shake the sleep from him, but still stumbled in a haze toward the door.

"Get your bearings first, Captain," a familiar voice said from the opposite corner of the room. Navas stood, put a book down, then came toward Searlus.

"How long have you been here?" Searlus asked.

"Wayfinder Hemol sent for me as soon as he left."

"It's getting bad, isn't it," Searlus asked.

"There's no going around it," Navas said. Then, he dropped his head. "We couldn't find him." Searlus put his hand up to silence his friend. He found himself counting planks on the ceiling. After a long moment, Searlus spoke.

"No captain talks about this part of the job."

"Doesn't matter what the job is if you aren't up for it," Navas said.

"I don't have a choice."

"If it's too much, then don't do it."

"I already felt like I have anchors tied to my ankles. The Coiled Whale, stranded at sea, the rescue, being captain, and now..." Searlus' voice trailed off.

"If there's anyone who can go out there and lead these men through the storm, it's you. You've always been a captain, only now it isn't on a rowboat in the pond behind your grandparent's place. It's a filthy Zamarian ship." He paused. His voice mellowed as he continued. "But we all have limits. Know yours. For all our sakes." With that, Navas clapped his friend on the shoulder and opened the door to the deck. Rain flooded in sideways, carried by the wind. A howl filled the cabin. Navas pushed the door shut, and relative calm fell over the room again.

Searlus stood by the double doors, trying to steady his breathing. His body was at peace, but his mind swirled like a flaming hurricane.

"You owe me one," Searlus said. "For what you let happen to that boy." He grunted one more time, pulled his cloak tight, and burst through the double doors.

. . .

With only half a crew, and now a man down, Searlus joined in with the preparations wherever he saw a need. He helped secure the rigging on the foremast. He carried the barrels of rum up from the dank lower decks and tossed them overboard. All the while he kept an eye on his men. He wasn't looking for anyone slacking off, the risks were too high right now. Even Kaius gave him a hand securing the freshwater barrels below deck.

Searlus was looking for the half-second flash of panic on the faces of his men when a crack of thunder exploded overhead. He looked into their eyes any chance he had, to find out who was best at hiding their fear. Every man on board was afraid. They all had been tossed overboard during the last storm, and here they were back into the proverbial fire, more ill-prepared than the first time.

Searlus was confident the Wavemaker would get them through this storm. He wasn't sure why, but the way the wind filled their sails with a steady gale, he was confident they could cut through the waves and make it to clear skies.

Searlus stood on the helm and surveyed the chaotic skies. It was dark, and the only light came from the lightning strikes. They were in the heart of the storm, though, which meant the lightning struck every few seconds. Searlus studied the clouds, noting which way they moved, then called out for the crew to alter course. He wanted to move in the opposite direction of the storm.

As he called out this order, a flash of lightning struck just overhead, illuminating the entire deck. Searlus saw a man crouched against the main mast with his arms wrapped around it as tight as he could. Searlus headed toward the man in an instant. The crew buzzed by him, back and forth, carrying out his last command. The ship was beginning to change course. Searlus touched the man's shoulder. The sailor turned and screamed. No one on the deck heard it. Searlus could see it was a man named Barnah. He motioned for the man to follow him. Barnah shook his head. Searlus crouched down and pulled the man over his shoulder. The next moment they were in the captain's quarters.

"Can't swim. No water. Not again. Can't swim. Can't swim," Barnah mumbled over and over. There was a loud hiss from the storm and then it was gone. Cora had stepped into the captain's quarters.

"Barnah," Searlus said. "Barnah," he said again, louder. The man kept mumbling, only now it was inaudible.

"Let me stay with him," Cora said. "I know the fear that's got him wrapped up." Searlus nodded and turned back to the trembling man.

"You're safe. Cora's going to stay with you until the storm has passed."

The mumbling man sat on a chair and rocked back and forth in silence. Searlus pushed his way back through the double doors into the storm.

Searlus felt something that he hadn't felt since before he left the captain's quarters after his nap. Raindrops smacked against his cheek only sporadically. The incessant drumming on the decks had ceased. The wind still roared, but the worst of it seemed to be over.

Then, with haunting similarity, the bow of the ship lurched forward, down into the sea. Another massive wave washed onto the decks. Searlus grabbed a nearby railing and held tight. Fear had knocked the wind from his chest. He would be the only one left on the ship. He knew it. The wave had taken them all.

He heard cheering.

Getting up to his feet, he saw seven men holding tight to one another, arms locked together, with one man holding tight to a rope secured to the foremast. Once the ship evened out, they let go and fell on their backs on the soggy deck. Moonlight peppered the sky as the storm clouds passed. Searlus approached them.

"Horah, Captain Searlus!" one of the men said.

"Horah! Horah!" they all said.

"You are the heroes of this day," Searlus said. "The sea is not our master!"

"Horah!"

"Ho!" a voice bellowed. "Look!" The men gathered near the starboard side and peered overboard. The young sailor pointed into the dark water. A glowing white blur swam lazily near their ship. Searlus pulled the Zamarian spyglass from his waist. The glass had been cracked during the storm, but he confirmed his suspicion.

Through the cracked glass the luneshark was magnified, and its dorsal fin bore the red slash of a small dagger.

"Follow that luneshark!"

# 21

## THE HUNT

The shark meandered through the water, apparently unaware that it was being hunted. Meanwhile, Searlus' crew had memories like the fish they hunted, forgetting the storm they had just survived, and now wholly focused on the task at hand. The sails were raised and the harpoons were brought to the deck. A rowboat was being loosed from its rigging.

"Navas and Kaius, grab an oar." Searlus knew his friend would love being part of the action, and that his enemy would hate having to be so close but only be an oarsman. Neither man said a word, they stepped silently into the boat. Searlus helped load the harpoons.

"You need someone who knows how to use those," an old voice said.

"Guessing you want to finish what you started?" Searlus asked. "If you're not too sick?"

"I think that poison has about run its course," Wayfinder Hemol said. He coughed violently as he stepped into the boat.

"You dropped the tarpon?" Searlus asked one of the sailors.

"Yes sir," he said. "The beast is circling it now."

"Good. Prepare another but hold until my signal."

"Yes, sir."

Searlus pulled his cloak from his shoulders, and stepped into the boat, his bare chest shining in the moonlight. A few Horak sailors began lowering the boat. Kaius started laughing as soon as they were below the deck.

"That shark's going to think you're looking to mate," he said.

"You really should take that cloak off more often," Wayfinder Hemol said. "Get some sun." Searlus looked at Navas, who only smiled and shrugged.

"That's my best cloak," Searlus said. "Can't risk it."

"No arguing with that," Wayfinder Hemol said.

"Are we going to talk fashion or kill us a luneshark?" Kaius asked.

"Waiting for you," Searlus said. Kaius huffed and grabbed an oar. It took him and Navas a moment to orient themselves to each other's rowing pace. Before Searlus finished tying a rope to a harpoon, they were circling the ship at an even pace. The two oars sliced into the water and pulled them along the surface in near silence. Searlus finished securing the other end of the rope to the small boat. He handed the harpoon to Wayfinder Hemol. "Want to finish what you started?"

"No, no," Wayfinder Hemol said. "Best if you get him hooked."

"It's your kill," Searlus said.

"It's our kill. For all Horaks."

Searlus nodded and tested the harpoon's weight in his hand. It was light. The barbed point was brown and rusted. Zamarian tools were always the cheapest. They couldn't get the best supplies. A flicker of empathy rose in him. He realized they couldn't get the best supplies because no one, even Horaks, would sell them the best goods, even if they could pay. The Zamarians were stuck in a downward whirlpool.

But, before that thought could find root, Navas whispered.

"Now, Searlus."

A dim mass hovered around the bloody bait. It's massive tail fin propelling it through the water with impossible force. The dorsal cut through the top of the water revealing Wayfinder Hemol's handiwork with the dagger during their previous encounter. A dark streak across the glowing skin. The beast swam toward the boat.

"Oars up," Searlus said. Navas and Kaius slid their oars out of the water and tucked them inside the small boat. The luneshark was right on them now. It's length from nose to tail dwarfed the boat, and Searlus had a vision of panic. The shark could simply bump the boat, or a rogue wave could come, and they'd be floating supper for the infernal beast.

Pushing the thoughts away, he raised the harpoon with the rope tied to the end, and just as the beast floated by, sent the metal weapon whistling through the water with all the strength he had left. It pierced the water with a splash. The splash was followed by an underwater roar. The beast kicked its tail and was gone.

Searlus' boat was being pulled behind.

"Hold!" Searlus said. The rope was pulled taut as the luneshark zig zagged through the water. Searlus murmured, "Don't dive. Don't dive." He heard Wayfinder Hemol mumbling something as well. He looked over and saw the old man holding his dagger at the ready.

"Think you're going to slice it up, old man?" Kaius yelled from the back of the boat.

"It's to cut the rope if she dives, you fool." Kaius didn't say another word. Searlus smiled as he grabbed another harpoon, this one free of any entanglements, and rose to his feet.

With his feet wide, he half knelt against the front of the boat with the weapon raised above his head. The beast swam back and forth in the dark, a shooting star in the midnight water. Searlus steadied his hand, waiting for the perfect moment that he knew would never come. Without thinking, he let the harpoon fly.

Miss.

It pierced the water beside the beast, and the beast continued its escape, giving no reaction to the harpoon.

"Again," Navas said, handing him another harpoon. Searlus repeated the stance, but his mind was as hazy as before. There was no clear shot. There was no confidence that he could strike this beast. He stepped down from the front of the boat.

"I can't," he said.

"Let me do it," Kaius said at once. He grabbed the metal weapon from Searlus and stood up on the boat. Searlus filled the seat where Kaius had been to keep the weight even. Kaius's arm rose too high, and after aiming for a split second, he let the harpoon fly. Whether he tried to throw the harpoon too hard, or he had terrible balance, Searlus didn't know, but when the harpoon splashed into the water near the luneshark another splash followed right after. Kaius had thrown himself off the front of the boat.

Searlus and Navas looked at each other in the moonlight and failed to stifle a laugh. They heard Kaius cursing in the distance as the luneshark continued pulling them forward. When they turned back to the front of the boat, the shadowed figure of Wayfinder Hemol stood with a harpoon raised high in his left hand. Tucked in his right arm were more weapons at the ready. Without warning, Wayfinder Hemol let the first harpoon fly.

The luneshark roared.

A second later another harpoon was raised high and loosed.

The luneshark roared again.

Wayfinder Hemol repeated this motion, over and over, Searlus and Navas supplying as many of the steel barbs as the Wayfinder needed. The harpoons continued to hit their target. The boat slowed and slowed. Wayfinder Hemol put a seventh and final barb in the back of the great fish, and the boat drifted to a stop. Wayfinder Hemol sat down in the boat. The belly of the shark breached the surface of the sea, and its glow rivaled the moon. Dark tendrils of blood floated out from the carcass.

Just then, a rhythmic chant rolled across the sea. "Horah! Horah! Horah!"

# 22

## ON ICE

The *Oathslaker* had been following behind the chase and took about an hour to catch up with the small boat. The dead luneshark was a submerged lighthouse for the boat, which made it easy to find the shark killers. Searlus, Navas, and Wayfinder Hemol rejoined the crew on the deck on the ship. Kaius sat near the rail soaking wet, with a towel wrapped around him. Searlus addressed the crew.

"This beast tormented Wayfinder Hemol and I when we were stranded at sea," Searlus started. He read their confused faces and clarified. "Yes, this beast. When we strip the meat, you'll see a slash on its fin where Wayfinder Hemol kept us from becoming luneshark lunch in the open sea. I'm happy to report it was Wayfinder Hemol who took down this beast. Not with a single blow, but with seven, perfectly placed harpoons. As you eat tonight, thank your Wayfinder."

Cheers rose from the deck. Searlus nodded to Wayfinder Hemol, signaling it was his turn to speak.

Wayfinder Hemol returned the gesture with a nod. The cheers died down and he spoke softly.

"All beasts belong to the Wavemaker. I take no pleasure in this killing. But I don't think it was without meaning. The Wavemaker requires the blood of a luneshark for entrance to Gildenwood. We have no High Captain among us to offer the sacrifice, and the journey to Gildenwood remains a difficult one. The storms have blown us far off course. Yet, it seems the Wavemaker is up to something. Take heart, Horak brothers. Take heart."

There was less cheering this time. A few sporadic claps that died down instantly. Searlus felt the tension in Wayfinder Hemol's speech. He wasn't sure if he should feel comfort that perhaps the Wavemaker was still moving among them, or hopelessness that they were nowhere near Gildenwood. It seemed as if the crew were feeling the same tension and were beginning to lean into the hopelessness more than Wayfinder Hemol had intended.

"Hop to it, then," Searlus called out. "I want everything up here but the bones. Take special care collecting the blood. Don't let any sea get in."

The men didn't hesitate. The small boat full of Horaks with knives and barrels was lowered into the water. Searlus made his way to the captain's quarters and got cleaned up. Navas and Wayfinder Hemol went below deck to do the same.

The dark night had turned to lavender twilight as the crew worked. When Searlus returned to the deck after a short nap, fully clothed and face washed clean, he found the men exactly where he'd left them. Boxes of luneshark meat was being hoisted aboard and transported below deck. The sailors walked slowly about the deck, but all smiled as they passed their captain. Searlus spotted Wayfinder Hemol looking overboard and joined him near the rail.

"Bigger than I thought," Wayfinder Hemol said when Searlus approached.

"I told the men to pull loose the biggest tooth they can find," Searlus said.

"Ha, my grandson will love that. Wouldn't believe me otherwise. Hard-headed kids."

"I don't know anything about that," Searlus said, trying to sound playful.

"The sea's a swift teacher," the old man said. "And you're a quick learner."

"Not quick enough." Searlus looked toward the bow. "She's also ruthless."

"I don't want to talk about it."

"Yes," Wayfinder Hemol said. "Of course, Captain."

"These men been working all morning?"

"Yes sir. And they'll keep working until there's not a single sinew left on those bones."

"They need rest," Searlus said. His gaze was fixed on the white bones floating in the water. The ribs of the beast reminded Searlus of the rickety, cube shaped fish traps he and Navas used to set up as boys. The blood had dissipated into the water, making the area around the corpse only slightly darker than the rest of the sea. "Let's feast tonight. Double portions. Let the men have their merriment. We sail north first thing tomorrow."

"Yes, Captain."

. . .

Searlus spent most of the day in the captain's quarters. He found a crudely made map of the Sea of Beasts, full of hand drawn markings and lettering. He spent a few hours trying to pinpoint their location, but even his best guess was a shot in the dark. In addition to the unreliability of the map, everything north on the map was marked *Neverthaw,* which Searlus had never heard of before.

Through the course of the day Searlus felt a wave of excitement and optimism. He believed the luneshark was their sign from the Wavemaker that everything would work out. Searlus thanked the Wavemaker and recited passages from the holy texts. Then, Jok's face flashed in his mind, and the sea rushed in to drown any hope that had sprouted within him. He paced around the cabin, cursing, yelling, collapsing on the bed.

When he woke this time, darkness filled the cabin. The near silence on the ship told him the feast had long been over. Searlus was glad. The men needed a respite from their work, from authority. Searlus still felt like one of the crew, but he knew those days were gone. Thoughts of never joining in the camaraderie of the crew weighed him down as he got out of bed and pulled on his cloak.

"Thoughts of a man with his feet in the sand," Searlus mumbled to himself. These worries felt trivial compared to the dangers they still faced. By all accounts, they would never make it to Gildenwood. Even if they did make it, they wouldn't be able to enter without a High Captain. And that's assuming the *Gildenglory* survived the storm, and the High Captain wasn't thrown overboard. Then, they'd have to sail all the way home with no rations and an exhausted skeleton crew.

Searlus took a deep breath, pulled his cloak tight around his waist, and pushed open the doors to the main deck. A frigid breeze filled his hood. A handful of shadowy figures patrolled the deck.

"Captain," a young man said as he passed.

"What is that stench?" Searlus asked. The man laughed.

"Luneshark tastes like the first Feast of Floats," the man said in a dream-like voice. "But it smells like the inside of King Tiveros' bum."

"Oh," Searlus said, caught off-guard by the irreverence. The man nodded and returned to his pace around the deck. Searlus eyed the dark void that was the front of the ship. He checked the rigging on the main mast, tested the sturdiness of the railing, but all along his feet carried him to that fateful spot. Before he knew it, he was standing at the foremast, boots in the last solid spot Jok's had been. He leaned his head against the mast and closed his eyes.

"It doesn't get easier," a voice said a few minutes later, startling Searlus from his silent mourning.

"Don't you sleep?" Searlus asked before opening his eyes. The low, raspy voice had become a comfort to him.

"I'm old. Old people don't need sleep. Captains do, though."

"Slept all night."

"Oh we know. Thought you were dead in there.

Might have to tie a rope to you next time you go to slumber in case we need to pull you out."

"I wish I could stay in there."

"You don't."

"We aren't going to make it."

"Didn't know you were the Wavemaker, now," Wayfinder Hemol said.

"We'll turn around at first light," Searlus said. "We might make it back to the Lightholm on the luneshark meat."

"Is that what you want?"

"I don't want to lose any more men," Searlus said.

"No captain wants to lose men," Wayfinder Hemol said. "Deaths at sea cut different than any other. You don't see it coming. There's no funeral. You share your last meal without even knowing it, then you can't even remember it. And your body and spirit can't keep up with each other. There's no time to mourn on a ship. There's always work to do. But your spirit knows there's something wrong. Something is missing. You keep on learning to walk like your legs are all tangled up."

"Then what?" Searlus asked.

"Then a wave comes and pulls you under, or you make it to shore. You learn to walk with a limp."

"That's terrible."

"It's still walking, though. Still moving forward." Searlus didn't reply. There was a long silence on the pre-dawn deck. Waves rolled and whooshed like the gentle breathing of a newborn. Wayfinder Hemol put his hand on Searlus' shoulder. "You're the captain, we do what you say. But as your Wayfinder, I don't think the Wavemaker is done with us just yet."

Wayfinder Hemol patted Searlus' shoulder twice before making his way back to the middle of the ship. Searlus ran his hand through his beard and looked up at the night sky. The next moment, Searlus was jolted forward as a dull thud came from the hull of the ship.

They'd struck something.

# 23

## THE NORTH

"Get a lamp over here," Searlus said as he peered over the side of the ship. A small light bounced across the dark ship until it came to Searlus and the group which had gathered around him. Searlus took the pole and extended the lamp out over the ledge. He felt two pair of hands grab hold of his waist. The paltry glow from the lamp did little to illuminate the dark water, but Searlus searched and strained trying to find the beast which had struck their side. He feared for another brush with the Coiled Whale and prayed it was only a luneshark. But he found no living thing in the waters surrounding the ship. He saw what had struck them but felt no relief.

A thick block of ice floated helplessly in the water.

From what Searlus could see, the huge block was the size of the captain's quarters. It bobbed up and down in the water like it was trying to resist being pulled down to Hadyl. Searlus pulled the lamp back on the deck and the orange glow painted many expectant faces.

"Was it the Coiled Whale?" one man asked.

"Another luneshark?" asked another.

"Shadelings from Hadyl?" a young Horak asked.

"Ice," Searlus said. "A block of ice." Murmurs rattled through the group. "We need to slow down, especially at night. That was just a warning. We don't want to hit one of those going full speed." The murmurs continued, and no one moved. After an idle moment, Wayfinder Hemol stepped forward.

"You heard the captain, step to it. Lower these sails, wake the rest of the crew. Bring this ship to a crawl before the first light of morning."

As the sun rose over the horizon, it caught a dozen or so blocks of ice and refracted the light in a hundred directions. The dark sea looked like the night sky, full of shimmering stars. The crew had succeeded in raising the sails, and now the *Oathslaker* crept through the primordial dawn.

"This is the way," Wayfinder Hemol said to the small group Searlus had gathered in the captain's quarters.

"We'll freeze to death," Kaius said.

"Why are you even here?" Navas asked.

"I asked him to come." Searlus spoke from the large captain's chair at the far end of the wooden table. Searlus could care less about Kaius' opinion, but he'd heard rumors of discontent among some of the Horaks, and he wanted to keep a pulse on things, so he invited their leader. "Is there another way?" Searlus addressed Wayfinder Hemol.

"Does this boat have wings?" Wayfinder Hemol

smiled. No one else did. Wayfinder Hemol repeated, "This is the way."

"How much food do we have left?" Searlus asked.

"About three weeks at regular portions, not counting what we can catch, of course," Navas said.

"Won't catch much up here," Wayfinder Hemol said. "Too cold for the tarpon. Everything else lives down deep. Our nets aren't long enough."

"Am I the only one who hasn't lost his mind?" Kaius asked with growing intensity. "We should have turned around a week ago."

"How much farther to Gildenwood?" Searlus asked. Wayfinder Hemol stroked his beard, opened his mouth to speak, then closed it. He spotted the map on the table and walked toward it.

"Hmm," he said as he ran his finger over the paper.

"This is Neverthaw, isn't it?" Searlus asked. Wayfinder Hemol chuckled.

"Best not let your father hear you say that word. That's Zamarian speak." Searlus felt a chill roll out from his chest to his arms to his fingers. Kaius smirked and shook his head.

"I didn't know," Searlus said.

"Ah, there's no harm in it, really," Wayfinder Hemol said. "Neverthaw, the Wild and Waste, it's all cold, bleak, hopeless."

"But it's the way?" Navas asked.

"Yes," Wayfinder Hemol said.

"How much farther to Gildenwood?" Searlus asked again. "The Zamarian map ends at Nev—the Wild and Waste."

"A few days at least. Could be a week or two. Longest it's taken is a month."

"A month?" Kaius repeated, standing from his seat. "These men won't last another week in these conditions. We must go home. We might not even have enough supplies to make it there."

"Sit down, Kaius," Searlus said. "I hear your concern."

"Then what are your orders?" Kaius asked.

"Would you speak to High Captain Kaphas in that tone?" Navas asked.

"This fool's not even a real captain," Kaius said pointing an indignant finger at Searlus. "Now you're comparing him to the High Captain? That's borderline blasphemy and you know it." Navas shot up out of his seat. Kaius did the same. The two men stared at each other across the table.

"Sit down," Searlus said. "I've made my decision." The two men looked toward their captain in surprise before getting back into their seats. Searlus let the silence build as he tried to find the courage to say what he felt to be the right course of action, even though it made little sense to him. He took a deep breath before speaking. "We're going to Gildenwood."

. . .

"If you're cold, rub the blubber from the luneshark on your skin to insulate yourself. Portions will be halved. Cora and Thea have agreed to help sew another layer into your cloak. Bring them whatever fabric you can find. We drop sails at first light, but only half of them. And at night we bring them up." Searlus stood on the balcony over the main deck and addressed the crew. Ice chunks clinked all around them. A cold fog escaped Searlus' mouth with every word he spoke. The Horak crew huddled together in groups wearing multiple layers. "I know it's cold," Searlus said. "But Wayfinder Hemol assures me we are on the brink of sailing upon Gildenwood's warm, calm waters. Hold tight, men."

Every day for the week after Searlus addressed the crew, more and more Horaks looked at their captain with furled brows. Fewer men spoke to him as he passed. Those who did speak to Searlus smelled of old fish, for these were the few who had decided to wear the luneshark fat on their skin. Each morning Searlus looked on the northern horizon for any sign of the fabled island, and each night he went to bed cursing the Wavemaker.

# 24

## THE FAR NORTH

They sailed farther north, through the light gray overcast days, and the dark gray, starless nights. Ice blocks littered the sea until the *Oathslaker* slowed to a near crawl as it cut through the gaps of broken glaciers. Another week had passed, and Searlus made the unpopular declaration to reduce meals to quarter portions. The number of crew members who met his eye became less and less with each passing day, until he spoke only with Navas and Wayfinder Hemol.

One impossibly cold night Searlus was on the late watch while the crew rested below deck. He wore his usual cloak, but under a few layers of Zamarian wool. His skin was rank with luneshark fat as he stood against the foremast, letting the thick wooden beam block the frigid wind. He turned when he heard footsteps behind him.

"You don't see that every day," Navas said with a smile.

"Zamarian wool is warm. Not going to apologize for

that," Searlus said as he pulled the hat down tighter over his ears. "And I never got that hat before we left."

"I mean the captain taking the late watch."

"Don't want these men thinking I'm above it. They'll turn on me in a flash."

Navas dropped his gaze to the wood-plank deck. There was a long pause before he spoke.

"Might be too late for that."

"What do you mean?"

"I just came from below deck," Navas said. "Kaius is getting everyone stirred up."

"A mutiny?" Searlus asked, turning toward his friend. Navas nodded in the moonlight.

"First thing in the morning. Kaius plans to address everyone from the helm, claim the captaincy, and set sail for home. Heard him talking about being the High Captain someday. Said this will help his cause when he returns home a hero." Searlus felt the blood drain from his legs. He slid down the foremast until he sat on the deck, back leaning to the giant pole. "I'm still with you," Navas said. "Wayfinder Hemol is, too. I think we could convince Barnah and Captain Zadoah, too."

"No," Searlus said. "It's over. And Wayfinder Hemol is looking sicker by the day. He needs medical attention."

"What?" Navas asked, kneeling on a knee near his friend. "It's not over."

"It's over, Navas. Let Kaius be captain. Might be the only way we touch the Isles of Hor again."

"But Gildenwood?"

"It probably doesn't even exist," Searlus said, his voice getting louder.

"What are you talking about?" Navas asked. "The sea's got you mad."

"When I fell overboard, I told the Wavemaker that I would serve him faithfully if he saved me," Searlus said.

"And?" Navas asked.

"And look at us," Searlus said, rising to his feet. "You think this is saving? This is torture. I wish the Coiled Whale would have wrapped its tentacles around me until my bones were sand. That would have been quick. Now we're sailing a stolen, desecration of a ship to our inevitable, frozen fate. The Wavemaker doesn't care about us!"

"Well I'm glad that beast didn't drag you down to the depths of Hadyl. I'd be a Zamarian pincushion if the Wavemaker hadn't spared you. Not to mention the pain of thinking you were gone forever once you fell overboard." Navas was nearly spitting as the disgust dripped off his voice. "And you of all people should know the pain of losing someone at sea."

The image of Jok standing on the bow of the ship flashed in Searlus' mind. His chest sank as the air crept out of his nostrils. He felt his legs grow weak again, but this time Navas' grabbed hold of him and slung Searlus' arm over his shoulder.

"Let's see how this ends," Navas said. "Together." Searlus regained his footing and stood with his eyes closed for a long while. After a long while he opened his wet eyes and nodded.

The sky was turning a dark purple as the first light of morning crept toward the horizon. The sound of muffled thunder echoed behind them. Searlus turned and found no clouds on the horizon, but the storm still grew nearer. Men clamored up the stairs to the main deck, filling the area with their cloaks and furs. In the morning light Searlus could see a single figure emerging from the doorway with a sword at his hip, and a swagger in his step.

Kaius made eye contact with Searlus and flashed a defiant grin before turning and making his way up to the helm. The Horak crew members diverted their eyes from Searlus, who stood on the forecastle watching the scene unfold. Kaius found his place at the front of the helm with seemingly divine timing as the sunlight broke over the horizon and golden light painted the ship. He cleared his throat to speak, but an old voice called out from the deck.

"Look!" Wayfinder Hemol shouted as he pointed toward the horizon. Every man on board looked over the deck and dropped their jaw at the sight.

Two golden suns were beginning to rise on the horizon.

# 25

## THE SECOND SUN

The crew sprang to life as if it was their first day at sea. Ropes whistled through pulleys and the thick canvas of the sails fell like thunder. Searlus stood at the bow and exhaled a deep sigh of relief. Searlus noticed for the first time in nearly ten days that when he breathed he couldn't see a wisp of cold fog in the air. In that same moment, a bead of sweat cut a path across his forehead, and down his temple. A smile broke upon his face like the first light of morning.

Men whistled and hummed the holy shanty as Searlus passed them on the way back to the captain's quarters. The revelry on the deck grew the closer Gildenwood appeared on the horizon. Searlus closed the door to the captain's quarters and took off his extra wool. Before he had a moment to sit and think there was a knock on the door.

"Come in," Searlus said. Wayfinder Hemol entered with a smile on his face.

"Can you believe it? You can't. You can see it and you

can't believe it. It's impossible. Yet there it is. On the horizon. Gildenwood. Gildenwood, my boy. Our heritage, and our future. Can you believe it?"

"I'm glad we made it," Searlus said, trying to keep his emotions subdued.

"Been twenty-eight years since I've last been here. Knew it would be my last time basking in the golden light in this life. Yet here we are. Sailing into the warm waters once again. In a Zamarian ship, no less! The Wavemaker is a mysterious one."

"What about the mutiny?"

"Haven't heard a word about it. Kaius' been uncharacteristically silent, too. The splendor of Gildenwood will do that."

"Can you get us in?" Searlus asked, a tremor of hesitation in his voice.

"No," Wayfinder Hemol said. His voice was just above a whisper. "You know that."

"There has to be a way."

"A way to go against the Wavemaker's decrees? Sure, we do that all the time. But this? This is different. Once our ancestors were cast out of Gildenwood, it's beauty and majesty remained cut off from all people. Only in recent years, the last four or five hundred, has the Wavemaker given us the instructions to enter again."

"And it has to be the High Captain," Searlus finished Wayfinder Hemol's thought. "I know I know. But there's a way."

"I've never been inside myself," Wayfinder Hemol said.

"That's a lie," Searlus said. "I trusted you. You said you've been here."

"I have been here. A few times. The High Captain only selects a few men to enter on a small boat. I was never chosen. What does that change?"

"You acted like you lived here. Like if we made it to Gildenwood everything would be okay. I thought you were just holding out on us. That you really could get us in, or that the Wavemaker would show up and make a harbor for us. Something. Anything."

Wayfinder Hemol chuckled. Searlus felt heat escaping from his cloak.

"Let's have this conversation after you've felt the glow of Gildenwood on your skin. Once you've heard the song of the golden seabirds. Then you can ask me if everything will be okay." There was a silence in the cabin. Then, as if on cue, a muffled Horak voice from the crow's nest called out.

"Land, ho!"

Searlus stood and was out of the captain's quarters in a flash. The air was warm and clean. He dropped his outer cloak as yellow rays washed over his exposed skin. The golden glow from the trees caused most of the crew to shield their eyes.

"It's always bigger than I remember," Wayfinder Hemol said, coming to Searlus' side.

"The trees," Searlus said. "They surround the island. We'll sail around and find an opening."

"Son," Wayfinder Hemol said, like a parent near the end of their wits. "The trees don't surround Gildenwood. The trees are Gildenwood."

"There must be beaches. Sand. Dirt." Wayfinder Hemol shook his head.

"The trunks go all the way down, breaching the surface of the sea, and forever down toward Hadyl."

"That's not possible," Searlus said.

"I didn't think you would be one to doubt the Wavemaker," Wayfinder Hemol said. Searlus stood at the edge of the ship, unable to shift his gaze from the shimmering sparkle of the golden leaves. A moment later, Navas joined the group and addressed his friend.

"The men are waiting for orders. Are we going in?"

Searlus turned to his friend, then to the old man nearby.

"Raise the sails. Let's get a good look at her."

Navas nodded, turned toward the deck, and began shouting orders. The crew woke from the spell Gildenwood had cast on them and got to work lowering the sails and preparing to circumnavigate this mysterious, otherworldly isle.

As the crew finished preparations, Searlus did something he'd always wanted to do, but had never gotten the chance. In a moment of inspiration, he realized that as the captain he could do whatever he pleased. So, he ordered the Horak keeping lookout in the crow's nest to come down, then he climbed the wood-plank ladder himself, until he made it to the top of the ship.

Looking around the cramped space, not much larger than the barrels he made, he secured his footing and got his bearings. A strong gust of wind washed over him, causing him to hang onto the side of the oversized wooden bucket. He closed his eyes in fear. The breeze passed as quick as it came. He opened his eyes and saw the men below deck, skittering about, making sure everything was in order. An all too familiar voice echoed in his mind, and he knew he'd made a mistake when he chose not to abandon the mission and get the men home safe.

Then, the trees came into glorious detail. The trunks golden, with deep grooves between the rough plates of bark. The leaves dangled on the edge of their branches, daring to soar off on the slightest breeze, yet remaining attached with some unfathomable will. But the thing Searlus couldn't wrap his mind around was the size.

They were about the distance from the shores of Tarsa to the Lightholm, but Searlus had already figured the trees rose higher than the crow's nest where he stood. Searlus remembered the pillars in the Lightholm's Gildenroom, and how naive he was to be wowed by that feeble extravagance. On the precipice of Gildenwood, the trees themselves looked nearly as thick as the entire Lightholm. And they went on as far as he could see. There were so many of these trees that there was no vantage point to peer through into the heart of the mysterious forest.

"What now?" the distant voice of Navas called out from below.

"Closer," Searlus called back. The bowsprit remained pointed toward the glowing isle. More and more trees came into focus. But the proximity brought torrential heat and blinding light. Searlus felt his skin growing tight on his face and hands. He realized his brow was furled and he was looking around in a perpetual squint. The sound of the crew thundering about the deck had slowed to an infrequent shuffling.

Searlus collapsed against the side of the crow's nest.

The wooden wall provided a brief respite from the unflinching heat. He was able to gather himself and a clear thought came to mind. He had to stop the ship.

He scrambled down the ladder and found all the men laying prone on the deck, debilitated by the heat. He hit the deck with a thud, skipping the last few rungs of the ladder. Bodies lay groaning in the heat as the ship sailed on toward the source of their pain. Searlus crawled up the stairs to the helm, the metal edging of the stairs burning his hands. Finally, the wheel was in sight, a collapsed Navas lay unconscious beneath. Searlus raised his hand and gave the wheel a spin before passing out.

# 26

## THE FOREST

"His time is up," Searlus heard a sharp voice piercing the darkness. His eyes were closed, and as his sense returned he felt a cool cloth on his forehead and the soft padding of blankets beneath him. "He could have killed us."

"I'm sorry," Searlus said in a low murmur. He opened his eyes and pulled the cloth from his head. Searlus could see darkness out the far window, but light shone in through the window by his bed. He guessed it was early evening. The three men who had become known as the captain's fist, Wayfinder Hemol, Navas, and Kaius were reclining on various chairs around the room. Searlus sat up slowly. "Just wanted to get closer. Is everyone safe?"

"Yes," Navas said.

"Barnah still can't see," Kaius said.

"It will return," Navas said.

"Maybe," Wayfinder Hemol said. "He will be fine though, yes. Better than fine, I'm sure."

"He's blind, old man. Some of us like to see," Kaius said before turning to Searlus. "And some of us would like to see Gildenwood. How do we get in?"

All eyes shifted to Searlus. Kaius' eyes were daggers, waiting in anticipation. Navas looked expectantly, ready to spring into action according to Searlus command. Wayfinder Hemol's head was cocked back slightly, his face was pale but welcome, like he knew Searlus' next words.

"We don't."

Silence. Only the sound of the floor creaking with the ebb and flow of the gentle tide filled the void. Then, a deep belly laugh filled the captain's quarters. Kaius spoke between his rolling laughter.

"You're through, through!" he shouted. "These men have put up with your negligence and mad-hattery for too long. You brought us here to look at it? Like it's some painting in the Saluman Gallery?" He laughed again. "Ha, you've killed us all."

Kaius pushed his way out of the room, his laughter growing hysterical. He slammed the door on his way out.

. . .

"I'm not a captain, that's clear," Searlus said from the helm. The entire crew stood huddled down on the main deck. Most were groggy, as Searlus was unaware it was the middle of the night when he called the urgent meeting. Darkness still filled the sky, but the light from his left still flooded the sea around them. Gildenwood continued to burn brightly it's golden hue, even into the midnight hour. "I'm not fit to be captain, so I'm stepping down from this role, and will appoint a new captain." A murmur swept through the crowd.

"But not before I say two final things. First, I apologize for my reckless command to sail into Gildenwood. Though we have the blood of the luneshark, we have no High Captain to offer the sacrifice. I did not weigh the risks, and my own desires clouded my responsibility to protect you all. I hope you will forgive me." Searlus looked out toward the group whose faces were partially lit by the leaves of Gildenwood and partially painted black with the shadows of the night. The crew was silent. "My last word as acting captain is this, I think we should stay."

Now, muffled conversations filled the air. The disgruntled men among the crew spoke openly to one another with loud voices.

"Hear me," Searlus said above the noise. "I'm putting it to vote. My proposal is to sail around Gildenwood for three days, like our ancestor Captain Hoshoah sailed around the Yariko Islands until they sank into the sea." The dissenters grew quieter. "If we can't go in, I want to see all sides of this mysterious isle. Let's take a vote. Who is in favor of sailing the perimeter for three days, and then returning home?"

The men, void of cloaks and any outwear, stood in the warm light. Many turned their head to look toward the spectacle, looking for an answer. After a moment, the first hand went up.

Wayfinder Hemol.

Then, another.

Navas.

Hands shot up sporadically after this initial momentum, until every hand on the ship was raised. Every hand except one.

Kaius.

"That settles it then. At first light, we drop sail. At the end of the third day, Kaius will be captain of this vessel."

. . .

Despite the late-night interruption, the crew were awake and preparing the ship before the sun broke the horizon. They worked by the light of Gildenwood, and had the sails lowered and secured at the break of dawn.

They sailed without complaint or grumble the entire day. Searlus helped the helmsman set a course on the outer edge of the Golden Zone, the name the crew were now using to refer to the proximity around Gildenwood where the heat was too strong to survive.

The crew worked hard, making sure the Zamarian ship sailed smooth. Searlus noticed every member of the crew kept an eye on the sacred isle, looking back and forth from their work, hoping to be the one to spot an opening or dock or anything other than an impenetrable wall of golden trees.

But there was nothing.

Shortly after the sun set, when he guessed they had circumnavigated the island, Searlus gave the order to drop the sails. The crew obliged, with a few grunts and sighs of disappointment. Searlus could read the emotions on the men's faces, because he knew his face shown the same.

Though he knew the code, that no one enters except the High Captain, he secretly hoped they had just reached Gildenwood on the wrong side, and that a cove would be waiting for them; that the Wavemaker would make an exception for them, because they had been through so much. He hoped for consolation for their woes, for losing Jok. But, as the last halyard was tied down, there were no openings.

The Wavemaker's code remained true.

The next day was nearly identical to the first. The crew rose early, set the sails, and they were off, cutting through the calm waters before the sun crossed the horizon line. They sailed along the edge of the Golden Zone, periodically veering closer to Gildenwood to test the heat, as if they couldn't remember just two days before when the heat nearly killed them all.

And, despite the facts, Searlus held on to an impossible hope that there was a cove or dock where they could enter, and that they might have just missed it the day before. The day went on, and Gildenwood remained a glorious, golden fortress.

That night, as the men were lowering the sails, Searlus found himself in the captain's quarters cursing the Wavemaker.

"You saved me from the Coiled Whale for this? For this disappointment? I would rather have died. The Coiled Whale dragging me down to the depths of Hadyl would be less torture than being so close to the only thing I've wanted, and yet seeing it dangling just out of reach. You are no provider, you are the ultimate trickster, tormenting those who serve you faithfully." Searlus was breathing heavy, but he saved his last breath for a burst of red-hot anger. "To Hadyl with the oath. I'm through."

As he stood, hands on the desk, head drooping low, he heard the door creak open, then shut.

"Get out," Searlus said.

"Brought you a salted flounder. The men are having a feast down there," Wayfinder Hemol said. A salt and spice aroma filled the room. Searlus' stomach growled. "Men are saying it's the best fish they've ever had."

"I'm not hungry."

"You're angry," Wayfinder Hemol said, his voice garbled by the food in his mouth. "Why?"

"Why?" Searlus said, whipping around. "We'll never make it home. All because of my desire to see this stupid isle, which just looks like golden horse dung from this far away since the cursed heat keeps us from getting closer."

"Ah," the Wayfinder said. "So you're angry at yourself."

Silence.

The Wayfinder continued.

"Did the Wavemaker go against his decrees? His code?"

More silence.

"You know the code. Who can enter, who can't. That hasn't changed."

"I thought–"

"You'd get special treatment," the Wayfinder finished the sentence. "No." He took another bite of the flounder before continuing. "You want the Wavemaker to let us in? That would be against his decrees and his code would mean nothing. Is that what you want, Searlus?"

"No," Searlus said.

"Right answer," Wayfinder Hemol said with a hint of finality. "Talk to the men. Their spirits are up. They have seen Gildenwood with their own eyes. The golden forest is burned into their imagination. No Saluman guard can take that from them. These men will hold fast to the way of the Wavemaker for all their days. I can guarantee you that."

Searlus considered the massive golden forest erupting from the sea and smiled. It was true. He had seen this sacred isle with his own eyes. The wonder of Gildenwood washed over him again. He thought about how he would describe it to his mother and father. He knew his sister would ask a million questions, so he would spend their remaining day making note of every small detail. As usual, the Wayfinder was right.

Just as Searlus was about to speak, to thank the Wayfinder, a low rumble echoed in the distance.

"It can't be," the Wayfinder said, moving toward the door.

"It's just a storm," Searlus said. The Wayfinder opened the door and motioned for Searlus to follow.

"There are no storms in Gildenwood."

# 27

## REUNION

The thunder grew louder. It wasn't until they emerged from the captain's quarters that Searlus realized the rolling thunder came one deep boom after another. One after another. Over and over in a rhythm.

"Drums," Searlus said to himself. Searlus' paltry crew had all abandoned their feast and stood on the edge of the deck, staring off into the distance toward the sound. Searlus joined the crew and looked out into the darkness, squinting to find the source of the drums. There was only darkness beyond the edge of Gildenwood's golden glow.

Searlus' mind raced as the low thump, thump, thump rolled over the still waters. Was it the Wavemaker's army descending from the skies? Only the Horaks knew the way to Gildenwood, so it couldn't be a human ship that had wandered this far north. And the drums. A ship lost at sea doesn't beat its war drums.

"Look!" Navas shouted from somewhere in the

crowd. All eyes followed the path of his finger. Searlus refocused his eyes on the black veil of night. Emerging from the darkness was the now unshrouded shape of two ships drifting across the surface of the water. A large, three-masted behemoth of a ship was heading straight for them. As it sailed closer to the light of Gildenwood, high above the main deck, attached to the highest point of the ship was a flag, tattering back and forth in the breeze.

A flag split green and blue with seven gold bars on one side and a gold circle in the middle.

"It's the *Gildenglory*!" someone said from the crowd. Cheers erupted from the deck. A few men broke out in an excited dance. Searlus stood awestruck. They'd stuck around, remained faithful, and the Wavemaker provided. These thoughts of thankfulness were short-lived, severed by the unmistakable sound of cannon fire.

The projectile splashed in the sea near the ship, spraying the decks with the warm saltwater. The men ran around reckless, like chickens breaking free from the coop. Another crack of the cannon, and this time the cannonball whistled by overhead before splashing into the sea. Men jumped up and down, waving surrender. They yelled and cried out, calling the High Captain by name, but the sounds of battle drowned out any hope of chivalrous contact.

"They think we're Zamarians," Searlus said aloud as he surveyed the chaotic ship. He looked up to the crow's nest, though he knew the Zamarian flag had been destroyed. He grabbed hold of a crew member and said, "Get me a white tablecloth."

"Yes, sir," the man said. The *Gildenglory* continued

to fire, and the men continued to run wild around the deck. Searlus stood still trying to take it all in, trying to think of his next move. He was determined to not blunder this moment, like he had on the approach to Gildenwood. While his mind raced through his options, a familiar tune filled the air.

"We sail on the surge of the raging sea, the ship the seed of the golden tree..."

Wayfinder Hemol's voice cut through the chaos. A few men stood awestruck nearby. They stared at the man with the same bewildered look as Searlus. The old man had finally lost it. In the face of an unfortunate death, he'd lost all grip with reality.

But, as Searlus stared, he heard a few other voices join the old man. The sacred shanty doubled, then tripled in volume as more of the crew joined. Before he knew it, Searlus found himself singing along.

"We trust our bowsprit unto thee, the Sacred Gale with us will be," they sang together. Their voices rose from the stolen ship and were swept across the sea on a midnight breeze. Another cannon fired. The men winced, a few silenced their voices, but others carried the tune. They kept singing, over and over they sang the holy shanty. Searlus figured, if nothing else, it would be a great way to die, with the sacred words on his lips.

The longer they sang, the more confident they became, and the louder their voices rang. After a few rounds, their tiny crew sounded like an entire battalion of Saluman guards chanting their pledge to King Tiveros. Their voices boomed over the sound of the waves. The creaking of the ship had vanished. They wrapped their arms around each other's necks, in a familial embrace, and sang. It was only these men, together, with the Wavemaker.

"Though the path you cut we cannot see, trust we will, and never flee."

And that's when Searlus realized the cannons had stopped.

. . .

"Yes, yes, we lost the *Gomoshah* in the storm, only the *Noak Tava* sails with us now, and that Saluman official must have fallen overboard, which no one was particularly upset about. That's old news, though. Tell us, how did you procure a Zamarian ship?"

Searlus' rag-tag crew from the Zamarian ship were seated at the head table in the galley of the *Gildenglory*, eating their fill of fresh flounder, and drinking wine from the vineyards of Kedess. The High Captain's question hung in the air as the crew, including Searlus, chewed their food.

"Searlus will share. He likes talking," Wayfinder Hemol said from the end of the table. "He was made captain of that vessel and led us here." He took a bite of flounder before continuing. "And led us on a luneshark hunt." The original crew of the *Gildenglory* gasped. "We've got two Saluman women on board, too." A few men spit their rum in surprise. All eyes shifted to Searlus, including the eyes of the High Captain and Captain Nimrad.

"This is true?" the High Captain asked. "You have the luneshark blood?"

Searlus swallowed then said, "Yes, sir. We have it. Wayfinder Hemol speared the luneshark."

"Wayfinder?" Captain Nimrad said with disgust.

"He was the only one who knew the way to Gildenwood," Searlus said. Captain Nimrad opened his mouth to speak but was interrupted by laughter and one man applause from the High Captain. He spoke over his own claps.

"Very good. Very good. Tell us all of it, starting with the moment you were thrown overboard. And get those women a proper room on the *Gildenglory*."

Searlus put down his food and took a drink of wine to clear his throat. The galley was silent, only the creaking of the ship dared interrupt the story, which was quickly becoming legend. When he finished, the High Captain clapped again, then dismissed everyone, telling them he had a big announcement first thing in the morning.

Searlus slept in his old hammock on the *Gildenglory*, below deck with the other Horak crewmen. The men kept asking him questions, wanting to know more details about the Coiled Whale, the Zamarians, and their ship. Searlus answered a few before waving them off to get to sleep. Once he shut his eyes, he fell right asleep.

He woke a second later.

"Main deck, now you foxes," Captain Nimrad shouted. The crew's quarters buzzed with energy. Searlus realized this was more than just not wanting to be the last man on deck. Yesterday was the first time these men had seen

Gildenwood. Searlus' men had spent three days basking in its glory. A pang of guilt for losing some of his awe and wonder grated against him as he walked the stairs to the main deck. He got in line with the rest of the crew, facing forward toward the High Captain, whose back was to Gildenwood.

"You all have weathered many storms to make it to these holy waters. Very few Horaks see the wild glow of Gildenwood. I doubt you will forget this moment," the High Captain said with his usual pomp and drama. "It is time to fulfill the purpose of our journey. I will select a small crew to bring me into the heart of Gildenwood, which we can enter because of the luneshark blood provided by Searlus' crew." Captain Nimrad's face wrinkled in disgust. "Once inside, I will make the sacrifice for all Horaks."

A buzz started in the group as the men expressed their excitement.

"If I call your name, go to your quarters and strip off all material from your body, clothes, jewelry, everything. Then, report to Captain Nimrad."

The buzz grew louder as the men whispered about the curiousness of stripping naked.

"Shoam of Betzur," the High Captain said. A bald man, not much older than Searlus, but almost a head taller, stood up straight, nodded to the High Captain, then disappeared below deck.

"Timoh of Shakum." A young man who looked like a near replica of the first, except with long dark hair, followed close behind the bald man.

"Searlus of Ramooth."

# 28

## THE BOAT

"**G**o get changed," Navas said. His elbow jabbed into Searlus' ribs. A million thoughts rang through Searlus' mind at the mention of his name. Had he heard correctly? Was there another Searlus aboard? Did that mean he was going into Gildenwood? Did that mean he would die?

All these questions, and more, continued to echo in his head as he descended the stairs to his sleeping quarters. He pulled off the silver ring his mother had given him on his twentieth birthday and tucked it into the boot he had just kicked off. His cloak was next.

Only a gold chain necklace with a circle charm on the end hung around his neck. The circle hung dead center of his chest. His father had given it to him nearly fifteen years ago when Searlus had started training to become a captain. There was a room on the ground floor of the Lightholm where these necklaces were made, and every Horak boy received one when they started their training.

Like every young Horak boy, receiving his necklace was the first time he had entered the Lightholm. He hadn't taken it off since that day, and he never guessed he would take it off to enter Gildenwood.

Now, he lifted the gold over his head, coiled it in his hand, and slid it into his boot.

"Put this on," a raspy voice spoke from behind him. Searlus jumped and turned to find Wayfinder Hemol standing in the hall outside the sleeping quarters holding a white linen cloak.

As Searlus emerged from below deck, the remaining crew members were standing together, watching something on the far end of the ship. One of the closer Horaks saw Searlus and moved out of the way. This caused a ripple effect as the crew split, allowing Searlus to walk down the middle. Searlus walked slowly through the group with his bare feet splashing in the puddles of the deck. At the end of his procession, he saw a small rowboat hanging over the side of the ship. Shoam and Timoh were loading it with supplies.

"Take a nap, did ya?" Timoh said. "We're nearly finished."

"Sorry," Searlus said.

"Get in, grab an oar," Shoam ordered. Searlus did as he was told. He grabbed hold of the rope suspending the boat in the air, then stepped up on the ledge of the ship. For the split second he stood there, he could see the sea splashing against the side of the ship two or three stories down. The memory of falling overboard and smacking the water flooded his mind.

"Go on," Shoam said. Searlus stepped over the space between the ship and the boat and secured himself against the side of the rowboat, near the opposite oar. A moment later Timoh joined and sat near the second oar. Shoam sat in the back of the boat, near a large rudder he could control by hand.

They sat suspended high over the sea in their little rowboat and Searlus lost track of time. He looked around the rowboat and found the seat in front of him was thickly padded purple linen. The back half of the boat had been stuffed with many trunks of gold coins. Since he had helped gather the coins from the side of the ship after they left the Lightholm, he knew this was only a fraction of the total. Still, he was sitting on a rowboat with more gold than he and Navas had made since they opened their barrel shop.

He had to look away, back to the deck of the *Gildenglory*. He saw Navas, with a huge grin on his face. Searlus shrugged and gave his friend a look of friendly panic. Navas mimed taking a deep breath and Searlus smiled and shook his head playfully.

Next he caught Wayfinder Hemol's stare. The old man stood toward the back of the group. "Don't die," he yelled. A few Horaks turned toward the old man, but Wayfinder Hemol just laughed to himself. Searlus couldn't help but join in the laughter. It ended abruptly when he caught Kaius' burning gaze.

The young man stood near the rail of the ship and looked with furled brow directly into Searlus' eyes. There was no hiding what Kaius was thinking. According to him, he should be the one sitting on the boat, wearing the white cloak, preparing to enter Gildenwood. Not the incompetent Searlus of Ramooth.

To Searlus' delight, the gaze was short-lived as the doors to the High Captain's quarters swung open. Two men exited the quarters, rolling out a purple fabric on the deck of the ship. High Captain Kaphas emerged on the purple path in a bright white cloak, adorned with jewels and gems of every color. Multiple gold chains hung from his neck, causing him to crouch ever so slightly under the weight. An oversized tricorn hat, it's brim lined with gold and a ruby at each point, sat snug on his head. He carried a small golden jar with both hands and walked slowly to the boat.

The purple fabric led up the stairs and over the side of the ship. The High Captain walked slowly up the stairs and sat on the padded chair. He adjusted his cloak and made sure the jar was safe in his hands. Once satisfied, he looked over the front of the boat, out toward the glowing, holy isle and spoke.

"To Gildenwood."

The small boat began to drift down toward the water. It took Searlus a moment to realize four Horaks stood on the edge of the ship, slowly feeding ropes into the pulleys. The downward glide was slow and steady. So slow and steady that Searlus didn't notice they had touched down onto the sea until Timoh splashed his oar in the water. Searlus felt a punch on the back of his shoulder from Shoam, who had his other hand on the rudder.

"Okay, okay," Searlus said placing the oar in the water.

"Silence," the High Captain said from the front of the boat. "Point the boat toward Gildenwood and tie your blindfolds."

# 29

## GILDENWOOD

Searlus looked to Shoam for direction, but he had already lifted a thick, white strip of cloth and tied it around his head, shielding his eyes. Timoh handed one to Searlus. He obeyed the unspoken orders without saying a word. As he pulled the fabric tight, the world went dark around him. Feeling around for his oar, he grabbed it and slid it down until he felt the resistance from the water. Then, he rowed.

A gentle breeze brushed across the exposed skin of his face as they picked up speed. The High Captain was murmuring something under his breath as the little boat cut across the water. Searlus continued to row while the memory of the intense heat burned in his mind. Shoam and Timoh hadn't experienced the heat before. He debated warning them, but just before he opened his mouth, he reasoned that the High Captain must know about the heat, and maybe he knew a time to enter when the heat was less.

Before they made it too far, a near flaming gust washed over the boat. Searlus' face and hands became dry and cracked in an instant. His mouth filled with invisible sand. The High Captain continued to murmur, seemingly unfazed. He could hear Timoh breathing heavy beside him. Searlus slowed his pace.

"Row!" the High Captain said. Searlus jolted upright, causing the boat to rock gently. "Let only death stop you," the High Captain said in a wild, manic voice. Searlus continued to row as the heat weighed down on him like the sun had just dropped in his lap.

Between the shouts and the splash of the oars hitting the water, a new sound grew in intensity. A rolling hiss filled the air, like they were entering the mouth of a giant snake. The hiss then mixed with an incessant popping sound. The boat began to rumble beneath him. Moisture dripped from his head and face. He licked his lips to keep them from cracking and tasted a bitter saltiness. The salt taste was more than just sweat. It was from the sea.

The sea was boiling.

"Row!" the High Captain called out again.

Searlus' mind could think of nothing but the heat. His arms were weak. The heat sucked up the moisture from his muscles. Somehow, he continued moving the oar back and forth, propelling the small boat through the boiling, hissing water. His throat was so dry he could no longer swallow. He thought of pulling the bandana from his eyes so he could see Gildenwood up close before he died, but his hands continued to row as if they had been melded to the oars themselves. He began to sway backwards and forwards, backwards and forwards. The thin cloak was sweat stuck to his back. And then, like waking from a bad dream, the heat was gone. The High Captain spoke.

"Take off your blindfolds and rest."

Searlus lifted his heavy arm to the back of his head and pulled the blindfold lose. It fell to his feet and Searlus blinked in the warm, soft golden light. He saw a canopy of golden leaves overhead before passing out.

. . .

"We sail on the surge of the raging sea, the ship the seed of the golden tree."

Searlus woke to the High Captain sitting on his padded chair singing the holy shanty and surveying the forest surrounding them. Sitting up, he could see Shoam and Timoh still passed out on the floor of the boat.

"First one awake, interesting," the High Captain said, looking over his shoulder at Searlus. "Welcome to Gildenwood, Son."

Searlus opened his mouth, but there were no words. The trees inside Gildenwood were solid gold, just like the massive trunks that made the exterior wall. Only now, the trunks were not distant, indistinct pillars, they were living, textured giants, and they went out as far as Searlus could see. The boat drifted slowly between the trunks. One was less than an arm's length away.

"Do not touch anything," the High Captain said without turning around. Searlus watched the tree float by. The bark had deep cuts and valleys forming a beautiful, golden pattern. That's when he remembered the pillars of the Lightholm.

"This looks like the Lightholm," Searlus said. The High Captain laughed.

"No, the Lightholm looks like Gildenwood. It was designed to be a set apart place, holy, like Gildenwood. I think you'll find many similarities." He paused. A shadow rolled over them. "And many differences."

Searlus looked up and saw a bird with multicolored feathers, a fanned-out tail, and a wingspan wider than the boat. It soared over them. Searlus stared and realized no two feathers were the same color.

"What is that?" Searlus asked.

"The names are lost to us," the High Captain said. A splash erupted from the still water and Searlus looked overboard. The water was clear as the air around them, now with a few ripples extending out into the trees. Swimming whimsical circles beneath the boat was a small school of golden angelfish. They were longer than Searlus' arm and stopped their play to look up at him. He felt a strange warmth rise from his skin, and realized he was not tired at all. His muscles were full of strength, and there was not a hint of drowsiness in him. The fish splashed again before swimming off between the trees, gold stones skipping between gold giants.

They drifted on and Searlus tried to stuff his eyes with the wonder of it all. Once the water settled from the fish, and became clear and undisturbed, he looked down the base of one of the trees, trying to see how deep the golden trunk went. There was no answer. The golden glow went down and down as far as Searlus could see.

A hollow thump from the middle of the rowboat startled Searlus. He turned and found an oval shaped ball wedged in the floor. He looked up and saw the golden leaves overlapping to create an impenetrable canopy. No sky shone through. Only glowing, golden leaves with the small ovals suspended from the branches. Some leaves rustled, and he saw eyes poking through.

"Eat," the High Captain said.

"What is it?"

"Again, we don't name it. But when the Wavemaker provides, you open your hands." Searlus picked up the fruit and felt the weight in his hand. The skin was smooth. He took it in both hands and pulled it apart. A thick, sticky juice flowed down onto his hands, and without thinking, he lunged forward and licked it up. His eyebrows raised and a childish smile stretched across his face at the taste of the sweet milk from within. He bit into the fruit without a second thought.

A yipping sound echoed in the tree branches above, and he looked up with bits of the fruit in his beard and saw a handful of small foxlike creatures with bushy white tails scampering off into the forest. The sound of the foxes woke the other two men in the boat.

"We're alive?" Timoh said, rubbing his eyes.

"Welcome to Gildenwood," the High Captain said. "Ready your oars."

Shoam and Timoh sat up straight, ready to row, but their eyes were trying to take it all in. Searlus heard Shoam fumbling over his words.

"Row," the High Captain said again.

Searlus dipped his oar in the smooth water, cutting through it like the sharpest knife filleting a tarpon. He guessed this was what flying felt like and envied the beautiful multicolored birds that soared overhead. The rowing was easy, in stark contrast to the blind straining and exhaustion on the flaming voyage from the ship to Gildenwood. Now, he was able to row at a steady pace, exerting almost no energy. And instead of darkness and death, there was light all around, coming from the trees themselves, which were full of wildlife of all sizes.

They rowed on and on and on. Searlus lost track of time. The trees were thick and innumerable. New species of animals appeared out of nowhere. And while it was just golden tree after golden tree, Searlus got the feeling he could stay here for a long time and never grow tired of it all.

After a long daydream of living in Gildenwood, the High Captain finally spoke.

"Sleep. We do it again tomorrow."

Searlus wedged himself against the side of his rowboat and closed his eyes almost instantly. There were no thoughts except Gildenwood. It was only Gildenwood. Golden dreams of this magical forest on the sea. Gildenwood through and through until he woke up.

"Is it morning?" Searlus said rubbing his eyes.

"There is no night here," the High Captain said from his chair. "No evening. No morning."

"Oh," Searlus said. He spotted more of the oval fruits in a small basket in the boat.

"Eat," the High Captain said.

"Where are we going?" Timoh asked just before he bit into the fruit with a crunch.

"I cannot explain it."

"Will we get there today?"

"As I have said, there are no days in Gildenwood," the High Captain said. "But there will be no question when we reach our destination."

"We sailed around the whole island in a day, before you all arrived," Searlus said to Timoh.

"This is not an island," the High Captain said. "These are holy waters. Time is not how you know it. We row on transcendent seas, where the water touches the Oasis. Where the Sacred Gale weaves between the leaves." He paused before continuing. "We will get there at just the right time."

Searlus didn't dare ask another question. He kept his oar moving at a steady pace, in time with Timoh, and they continued to cut their way through the trees. After long periods of rowing, they would sleep, wake full of energy, and do it again. The oval fruits were always spilling over the basket, and Gildenwood continued to go on forever.

They repeated this wake, row, sleep pattern over and over. Searlus knew they could have circled Gildenwood multiple times with the distance they covered. Still, they were in the heart of the golden forest, with no destination in view. After the seventh wake, and after a substantial fruitful breakfast, they rowed for hours until the trees stopped. Searlus looked over the shoulder of the High Captain and saw a clearing up ahead. Without speaking, he and Timoh rowed faster toward the clearing.

"Easy," the High Captain said. "We're approaching the Harbor Stone."

"Like in the Lightholm?" Searlus asked.

"A mere imitation. This is the original," the High Captain said. "Now, prepare the sacrifices."

# 30

## THE HARBOR STONE

Searlus and Timoh pulled their oars into the boat. The boat continued floating slowly toward the giant, gray, round stone in the center of the clearing. The surface of the stone was flat and larger than a house. The surface looked smooth, without a scratch or nick, and the edges were black like the outside of a cooking pot.

Shoam gathered the sacks with the sacrifices and passed them forward. Searlus passed three cloth bags full of gold coins forward without a second thought. The abundance of gold in Gildenwood, from the trees to the leaves, and even the fish, had stripped these coins of their appeal. There was no envy or desire for the gold. There was no fleeting thought of pocketing the coins, even though a single sack held more than he would make in years. There was no lack in Gildenwood.

As Searlus handed the last of the gold forward, the wooden rowboat hit the edge of the stone with a gentle thud. For the first time in what Searlus guessed was a week, the boat had stopped. Searlus shuffled in his seat, preparing to get out to help unload before the High Captain spoke.

"Only the High Captain can touch the Harbor Stone."

Searlus leaned away from the stone, less than an arm's length from where he sat. The High Captain stood, causing the boat to rock back and forth. Searlus leaned toward Timoh to avoid accidentally touching the stone as the boat rocked under the High Captain's movement. Finally, with a balance Searlus had yet to see in the High Captain, the man in the royal cloak stepped out of the boat and onto the stone. The boat steadied itself now that the disruption had been removed.

The men in the boat watched in silence as the High Captain walked toward the center of the stone. He shuffled along, not picking up his feet, slower than a calf learning to walk. He held luneshark blood in front of him, both hands wrapping around the gilded jar. As he reached the middle of the stone, he knelt and placed the jar in the dead center. He turned and made his way back to the boat.

Searlus had many questions, but he had enough social awareness and reverence to the Wavemaker to know this was not the place. There were no words spoken. The three-man crew on the rowboat did not talk, and the High Captain did not speak to them. He only repeated the same action over and over. He would come to the boat, grab a sack of gold, spread it around the perimeter of the circle until it was empty, then return and do it again with the next sack.

There were only three sacks, and although they were large, Searlus figured it would not take long for the High Captain to arrange them around the circle. But, when he began placing the coins one at a time around the circle, Searlus decided to make himself comfortable.

The sound of birdsong and foxtalk filled the forest around him with an effortless melody. He leaned over the side of the boat and looked down into the water, trying to see the bottom of the stone. But, like the trees, the base went down and down as far as he could see. Even though he couldn't see the bottom, he did notice something else as he stared into the clear water.

The water in the clearing was still and pure, just like all the water in Gildenwood. Only now, there were glints of gold floating around in it. The gold dust moved effortlessly through the water, shining like distant stars. Searlus realized he could see farther down into the water as well. There was more light getting in. He looked up and for the first time since they entered Gildenwood saw a patch of sky above them. A white, cloudless sky shone bright high above them, directly over the stone. Light poured in through the hole, extinguishing every shadow, every nook.

Searlus looked down to the High Captain who was just finishing arranging the first bag of coins. He took a deep breath and sat patiently, watching the High Captain return to the boat, grab another sack, and place the coins, one by one, flat around the stone.

Searlus lost track of time, but he guessed he could have made five or six barrels in the time it took the High Captain to arrange the three bags of coins around the circle. Finally, the last coin was placed and the stone looked like the patterned shell of a huge turtle. The High Captain returned to the center of the stone.

The three men in the boat watched with teeth clenched as the High Captain picked up the jar and began muttering under his breath. Searlus couldn't hear him but recognized the tune of the holy shanty. The High Captain dipped his hand in the jar, and when he pulled it out his fingertips were stained red, dripping with the blood of the luneshark. He flicked his fingers, and the blood splattered over a small section of coins. He took a step and dipped again. More blood coating his fingers. More blood dotting the stone, the coins. Again and again he did this, covering every coin, murmuring the holy shanty.

Searlus knew this was the last step of preparing the coins for the sacrifice. A sense of pride swelled up in him when he remembered that it was his crew that had hunted and killed the luneshark. They wouldn't be here if it wasn't for them. But, before he swelled too big, he remembered the reason the Wavemaker requires the blood of a luneshark, according to the holy texts.

The blood of a luneshark represents the union of Horaks and the Wavemaker. The Horaks had to put in the work, had to prepare, had to be ready and willing to hunt the large fish, but it would all be in vain if the Wavemaker did not provide the luneshark to be sacrificed. The blood being splattered on the sacrifice showed that the Horaks wanted to please the Wavemaker, they were willing to work for it, and that the Wavemaker wanted to partner with the Horaks.

A sense of peace filled Searlus. A peace flowing down from the union he had with the Wavemaker. He was about to forgive the Wavemaker for allowing him to be thrown overboard, and for losing Jok, but he locked eyes with the High Captain and a sense of fear made him shiver.

The High Captain had finished flicking the blood on the coins and was now looking toward the boat. He locked eyes with Searlus and a manic smile stretched across his face. He dipped his hand into the jar one more time, and flicked blood on his face.

A moment later a pillar of fire flashed down through the opening and covered the surface of the stone, including the High Captain. The sound like the most terrible windstorm filled the clearing, silencing the noise of the wildlife. The flames singed the edge of his cloak, and he felt the boat start rocking. Timoh was crying and shaking and shuffling around. The boat thrashed wildly. Then, a voice boomed from high over the opening in the canopy.

*"As sure as the waves beat against the shore, so does the Wavemaker keep true his word. The last great captain has set his anchor, a fish among you, filleted, but severing all nets."*

The voice was too much for Timoh. He stumbled over the edge of the small boat, disrupting the balance, which then caused Searlus to over adjust, causing the boat to flip. All three of the Horaks sank into the water as the flames burned on the surface.

# 31

## THE MIST

As the water engulfed him, Searlus was taken back to the night he was thrown overboard. A chill of panic shot through his body as he pulled his arms and legs into his chest like a baby in the womb. Instead of prolonged fear and uncertainty, darkness and cold, imminent death and Hadyl, Searlus opened his eyes and saw a comforting brightness all around. Shoam and Timoh thrashed in the water before the same peacefulness fell upon them, and their bodies relaxed, their limbs floating outstretched.

The pang of panic was washed away by the warm waters. The fire continued to burn overhead. Searlus got the feeling that nothing had ever died in these waters, and he was not going to be the first. He kicked his feet and splashed through the surface of the clear pond. He wiped his face, and when he blinked his eyes open, the fire was gone.

A thick gray mist covered the surface of the stone. The glow from the trees refracted the light a million ways, making it impossible to see into the haze. Shoam and Timoh surfaced shortly after Searlus.

"High Captain Kaphas!" Shoam said. His voice echoed through the trees. A flock of tiny birds, the size and color of a pear, scattered from a tree overhead. No voice returned his call.

Searlus kept his eyes on the Harbor Stone, waiting for the mist to clear. The look the High Captain had given him right before the fire was one of confidence. It was the shoulders back, chest out kind of look from a man who has done this before. Moments later, a shadowy figure of a man began to emerge from the heart of the mist. Searlus braced himself to see the burnt remains of the High Captain. But, when the High Captain finally stepped out of the mist and into the light, not a single part of his body had the slightest burn. Not a hair was singed.

The gold chains that hung from his neck were gone. His hat, with rubies and gilded seams was gone. His hands were bare of any rings. He stood on the edge of the stone, wearing only the white cloak, identical to the one Searlus wore, holding his hands behind his back.

"Help us," Shoam said to Searlus who turned to find the two other men working to turn the boat right-side up. He swam over to the boat and the three of them managed to set it right. Searlus had to swim back toward the edge of the clearing to get his oar. As he returned to the boat and climbed in, he turned to the High Captain who remained unmoved. His hands were still clasped behind his back, and his eyes were closed. Searlus and

Timoh began to row while Shoam guided them to the stone.

They slowed and came to a stop on the edge of the stone in front of the High Captain. He stepped into the boat and sat in his chair, not making eye contact with anyone. He pointed in the direction from where they had come, and Searlus and Timoh began rowing.

After a few moments of rowing, the clearing was behind them, and they were back in the thick of Gildenwood, trees all around. Shoam snaked the boat in and out of the trunks, trying his best to keep the bow pointed in the direction the High Captain had commanded.

Despite rowing for a few hours, Searlus' felt strong. His cloak had dried, and his muscles were loose. The wooden handle of the oar was soft in his hand. He wondered if they would row for multiple days, and if his body would be able to handle it. He knew he would get tired soon, but he had to row until the High Captain told him otherwise.

To pass the time, he would find a large tree, watch it come into view, and then track its trunk as far down into the water as he could. He had just finished following a particularly large tree, half the width of the Lightholm, all the way down into the depths of the sea, when he looked up to find the next tree to size up. For the first time, a blue clearing began to splinter through the forest.

Timoh increased his rowing speed, which caused Searlus to match it. He rowed and rowed and the blue grew and grew until Searlus realized they were coming to the outer edge of Gildenwood.

"The heat," Shoam said to himself from the back of the boat. Searlus and Timoh pulled their oars from the water at the thought of what they endured, blindly, upon their entrance. But before the last drop of water dripped from Searlus' oar suspended over the surface of the sea, the High Captain spoke.

"Row. And don't stop until we reach the *Gildenglory*."

Searlus made eye contact with Timoh, who only shrugged. He turned back to Shoam who had his jaw clinched and pointed to the water where the oar was supposed to be. Searlus obeyed and stuck his oar in the water, and they moved closer and closer to the edge of the tree line.

In a matter of minutes, they reached the tree line and burst into the open sea. Searlus could see the *Gildenglory* in the distance. His skin began to heat up and he took a deep breath to ready himself for the second round of unbearable heat.

It never came.

There was an intense heat, compared to the cool breeze of Gildenwood, but this heat was only the typical clear skied, unrelenting sunshine kind of heat, not the tree-emanating, golden, insufferable kind they had encountered on their journey into Gildenwood.

They reached the hull of the boat and the ropes were waiting for them. After securing the ropes, the crew pulled them back up to the main deck. The High Captain was the first to step foot on the deck. Captain Nimrad led the way back to the High Captain's quarters before Searlus, Timoh, and Shoam had time to exit the small boat.

The entire crew of the *Oathslaker* was among the *Gildenglory* crew, standing in complete silence. Searlus stepped off the boat and saw Navas standing a few rows back. The crowd of Horaks parted as he walked toward his friend.

"I've got a story for you," Searlus said with a laugh.

"Your face," Navas said, eyes wide as the moon.

"Yeah, haven't slept much," Searlus said.

"It's glowing."

# 32

## THE RETURN

Before Searlus could reply, Captain Nimrad stepped through the doors of the High Captain's quarters holding a small sheet of paper in his hands. The men turned in attention. He began shouting, despite the entire crew tightly packed on the deck.

"By order of the High Captain, many of you have been reassigned."

A collective groan sounded from the deck.

"Captain Zadoah is now the captain of the Zamarian vessel, and here are the men who will join him." He took a breath and looked down at his paper. He read twenty names aloud. Navas was last. Then he looked up and dealt a demoralizing blow. "The High Captain wants us to make it back in double-time. We're leaving. Now. Drop the sails."

. . .

After the flurry of activity from men running down to their quarters to get their personal belongings before going to the Zamarian ship, and after the unspoken complaints had mostly ceased, and after the sails had been dropped and secured and the ships were zipping across the surface of the nearly frozen sea, Searlus found himself sitting alone in the galley, picking at the remains of a flounder.

The High Captain burst in, humming a dirge with a golden chalice in his hand. He pranced around the tables, taking another drink between verses. He plopped down at the edge of a table and spoke to a group of young Horaks finishing their dinner.

"They said we were lost." His voice was loud and loose. "We made it. We did it. Gildenwood, my boys! I was there. The Wavemaker accepted my sacrifice. They said we were lost!" He wrapped his hand around one of the young men's necks and laughed. Then, after dancing around and whistling for a bit longer, he disappeared from the galley, and the Horaks returned to their silent meal.

This was a common occurrence for the first couple weeks of their return voyage. One night, once they were nearly clear of the frigid Wild and Waste, the High Captain got so drunk he passed out in the crow's nest of the *Gildenglory* and Captain Nimrad ordered the two closest men to carefully carry the limp body down the mast with a rope and pulley. That night, the men of the *Gildenglory* hailed those on the *Noak Tava* and the *Oathslaker*, and they lashed the three ships together for the evening, to share a drink with the men who had been demoted to the other ships. Searlus and Navas grabbed a pint of the Zamarian rum and sat against the rail on the bow of the *Oathslaker*, which had been mostly abandoned. Searlus told his friend about the journey into Gildenwood, sparing no detail. Navas peppered his friend with questions.

"You think it was the Wavemaker?"

"Who else could it have been?" Searlus asked.

"The High Captain?"

"No, no way. I've heard plenty of his carrying on to recognize his voice. It came from the fire. I'm telling you."

"The last great captain has set his anchor," Navas said to himself, repeating the Wavemaker's words. "Is that in the holy texts?"

"That was my thought, too. But it's not. Far as I can remember, it's not."

"That's unbelievable," Navas said. He took a drink of his rum and smiled. "If I didn't know you, I'd say you're a lying Saluman slug."

"I feel like a lying Saluman slug saying it out loud. Like it's the worst heresy."

"What'd the High Captain say about it?"

"Nothing," Searlus said, looking over to the illuminated windows in the captain's quarters of the *Gildenglory*. "He's been drunk since we returned to the ship."

"Zamarian rum," Navas said, lifting his cup.

"Maybe," Searlus said, shifting his gaze back over the water. There was silence as the boats rose and fell on the chest of the breathing sea. Searlus' mind drifted toward home. But Navas' next question unsettled him.

"What if the voice was true?"

"Talking about the Mistrider?" Searlus asked. Navas nodded. "Best to put those thoughts away. What my dad says anyway."

"What if this is the time? We've been waiting for how many generations?"

"I don't know."

"The Saluman Empire will bow the knee to the Kingdom of the Wavemaker, led by the sword of the Mistrider." Navas was standing now. He walked back and forth across the damp wooden floor. "That's what the voice meant. It's so obvious."

"You weren't even there," Searlus said with a laugh.

"Bet the High Captain thinks the voice was talking about him, that narcissistic clam," Navas said.

"That explains a lot." Searlus thought back to the drunken nights. The High Captain must have been celebrating his new appointment in service of the Wavemaker, ordained by the Wavemaker himself. "Say the High Captain is the Mistrider, what do we do?"

"Whatever the High Captain says, unfortunately," Navas said. He sat back down against the edge of the ship wall, facing Searlus. "What else?"

"That's what I'm afraid of," Searlus said. "It's too much. I just want to get home."

"Yeah," Navas said, his mind somewhere else. There was a short pause before Searlus saw his friend smile in the moonlight. "Guess I'm ready to see Devora, too."

"Keep it up and I'll throw you overboard and say you were drunk," Searlus said.

"You're not captain of this vessel anymore," Navas said. "Bet she's been thinking about me."

"That's it," Searlus put his cup down and started to charge Navas, who set down his own cup and rolled up his sleeves. Searlus flashed a smile before leaning back against the wall. "I'm too tired," he said as he sat back down.

"I'll be sure to tell her that her brother almost defended her, but he was too tired."

"Someone needs to," Searlus said, his voice trailing off.

"What do you mean?"

"You saw her in the market. Looked like a vagrant."

"She looked happy to me. Eyes bright."

"Stains in her dress. Hair falling out."

"She's a woman without a husband. And she won't take one. She's doing good."

"She's been listening to that magician from Kedess."

"Oh," Navas said.

"Exactly. She believes him, too. I'm losing her, Navas. Dad pretty much does his own thing. Mom doesn't care about anything, not really. She's the only family I've got."

"Ahem," Navas said.

"Blood family," Searlus said in response.

"Better than only having to worry about keeping headstones clean." Searlus didn't reply. There was nothing to say. He knew his friend meant no harm, and he hoped Navas knew he didn't mean to offend him.

Navas' statement hung in the air like the late-night

fog descending on the ships. The distant melody of the holy shanty flowed from the *Gildenglory* as a chorus of Horaks celebrated together. Searlus tried to find the words of apology, but before he could, Navas spoke again, without looking at Searlus.

"I'm going to sell the business."

"Our business?"

"Yes," Navas said. "I'm tired of it. We're just supplying the bucket the Saluman's use to haul our money and goods away to the palace. I won't do it anymore."

"Seems like we should talk about this," Searlus said, trying to keep the anger out of his voice. "It's not just your livelihood."

"You'll be fine," Navas said in an apparently more apathetic way than he intended. He quickly followed it with, "The High Captain likes you."

"What does that mean?" Searlus asked.

"Means you'll be working in the Lightholm when we get back if you don't screw it up. And where does that leave me? My barrels always leak."

"How'd you hear that?"

"My word, Searlus. Look around. He picked you to go into Gildenwood. Act right and you'll be the first mate before you're thirty-five."

"That's not…" Searlus started at rebuttal, but visions of him working and living in the Lightholm filled his mind. It felt right.

"You're not working there yet, golden boy," Navas said with a laugh.

"What will you do?"

"Barnah says old Migdah is about to retire."

"I thought he would die up there," Searlus said.

"Me too, but that's the word. And, Barnah says he'll put in a good word for me."

"That's what you want?"

"Yeah."

"Well look at you, the future Nightwatcher of the Lightholm. Keeping the sacred flame burning."

"Ha," Navas laughed. "That's nothing compared to the future First Captain of the Lightholm. You'll be my boss. That'll be a switch."

"Let's see how it feels," Searlus said. He finished off the last of the rum in his cup and extended it toward his friend. "How about you go get me a refill?"

"In your dreams," Navas said. But before he could say another word, a loud drum pounded three times, followed by a loud call from the *Gildenglory*.

"All hands on deck!"

# 33
## DOWN TO HADYL

Despite the theatrics, there was no immediacy to the call for the crew to return to their posts. The High Captain had sobered up and asked why they were not moving. Captain Nimrad made the orders. The crew returned to their assignments, lowered the sails, and the ships sped off into the black night.

And that is how they continued for weeks.

There were no rests. Breaks only for sleeping and eating. The already sea-beaten crew were pushed past their limit. Many spent their days and nights in their hammock, too sick to move. No amount of shouting or threat of withholding food would make the men move. With each passing sunset they withered away a little more.

Since the crew had spent much time together, facing storms, sea monsters, abandonment, ice, and Gildenwood, most were sympathetic to the sick. The more men who were hammock-ridden meant a heavier workload for those who could stand on their own. Still, despite Captain Nimrad's orders that only the working received their meals, the Horak men smuggled scraps of tarpon to their sickly friends.

And, despite his relentless optimism, Wayfinder Hemol was among the fallen. His old, frail body had been pushed to its limits as the luneshark poison coursed through his body. Searlus had taken it upon himself to care for the old man, doing both of their work, and bringing most of his meals down to his quarters.

"You eat it," Wayfinder Hemol said in a hollow voice. He hung in his hammock just above the floor, like a caterpillar in stasis. All the sick had been moved to the same room. The only light source came from the lamp Searlus brought with him. He couldn't see any other faces, just floating black sacks, like a cave of oversized bats.

"I'm fine," Searlus said. He now had to pull the rope around his cloak extra tight to keep it secured to his waist.

"Eat, boy. You'll need your strength for the Lightholm."

"You've lost it, now," Searlus said.

"Don't play coy. I know you've heard the whispers. The High Captain will pick a few from this journey to apprentice with him in the Lightholm. To be his aide. It will be you."

"Do I have to?" Searlus said without thinking.

"You don't have to do anything," Wayfinder Hemol said. "That's why you're here, though. Right?"

"I guess so."

"If you take it, remember the High Captain is just a man. We serve the Wavemaker." He was leaning forward now. He grabbed Searlus' cloak. "Don't forget that." Searlus nodded in the darkness. The old man's eyes were sunken deep into his head, like a corpse talking in the darkness. "Good."

"We'll get you to the healers when we get to the Lightholm. First thing."

"Ah," Wayfinder Hemol said, sitting back in his hammock. "Don't worry about that."

"We're close. We must be."

"Ha, and I'm supposed to be the Wayfinder," the old man laughed. "You've got good instincts. My guess is that we'll pass Salumoor tomorrow or the next day."

"Then we'll be home within the week. Hold on until then, okay?" Searlus stood and gathered his things. "I'll bring you more food in the morning."

"Yes, sir," the old man said. "And Searlus?"

"Yeah?"

"Though the path you cut we cannot see, trust we will, and never flee."

"Horah, Wayfinder Hemol."

"Horah, Captain Searlus."

. . .

Searlus went to bed that evening and woke to the call that confirmed what Wayfinder Hemol had said the night before.

"Land, ho!"

Searlus, and every member of the crew who could

stand, rushed to the deck at the news. They had reached Octav's Channel. In the morning sun Searlus could see the city far down the valley. While the others clamored for a glimpse at the great city, Searlus retreated to his sleeping quarters to prepare for the day. The shine of the spires, and the magnitude of the statues, were child's toys compared to the splendor of Gildenwood.

All day long, as Searlus was checking the integrity of the foremast halyard and cleaning the deck to prepare for the arrival to the Lightholm, his mind was filled with thoughts of his sister. Once he started in the Lightholm, he'd have the funds to help Devora get her own place. She could get a good job. His mom wouldn't have to work anymore either. His thoughts of charity quickly devolved into visions of grandeur at what it would be like working in the Lightholm. He envisioned himself sitting in the library near the top floor, dressed in a thick cloak, drinking wine, and discussing the finer points of the holy texts.

Then, as the sun was setting, Captain Nimrad called for the sails to be dropped, and for the Zamarian ship to be brought close and lashed to the *Gildenglory*. He called the crews of both ships together.

"Take anything useful that does not bear the Zamarian mark. Bring it aboard the *Gildenglory*. Then send that wretched vessel to Hadyl."

Searlus went aboard the Zamarian ship, and with Navas' help, carried a few barrels of ale back to the *Gildenglory*. After an hour, the *Oathslaker* had been sufficiently pillaged. A few Horaks readied a cannon. The High Captain emerged from his quarters and walked to the giant weapon. He struck a match and lit the fuse. An impossibly loud crack sounded, followed by a million smaller cracks as the steel ball forced its way through the hull of the ship. The Horak men readied another cannonball, and the High Captain fired again. After three strategically placed cannon balls at point blank range, the Zamarian ship began to take on water. The High Captain stepped away from the cannon and faced the full crew.

"Begin preparations to dock at the Lightholm."

# 34

## THE FOG OF HOR

As they continued to sail south, a thick fog began to swallow them up. In darkness, they had only their lamps to guide their way. In the fog, two men could stand on the stern of the ship and the tip of the bowsprit could not see each other. Captain Nimrad broke the ominous silence.

"Lower the sails." The crew did as they were told, in half the time, now with a semblance of a full crew aboard. "Stay alert."

"Where's the Lightholm?" someone asked. Captain Nimrad snapped his head to the sound of the voice, but there was no pinning it on a single man. The fog and the crowd kept the Horak's identity anonymous.

"Hold your tongue, all of you," Captain Nimrad said after searching fruitlessly for the offender. "Does anyone want to stand up here and make any other blasphemous claims?"

Silence.

"Get to your posts and await my orders," Captain

Nimrad said, nearly spitting. Searlus returned to the bow and checked the halyards yet again. They were taut, and ready to hoist the sail up on the foremast at a moment's notice. But until the call came, he stood looking out into the fog, trying to make out any familiar dark shapes against the even darker night. The ship sailed slower than a rowboat, gliding over the surface of the black water. The few lamps on the ship provided little light against the darkness invading.

Searlus heard a call that made his heart sink.

"The Lightholm!"

He turned toward the voice, scanning the sky for the blazing signal fire of home.

There was only darkness. Darkness opening up to darkness. The fog cleared for a moment, and Searlus felt an otherworldly chill through his entire body.

The dark silhouette of the Lightholm stood in contrast to the gray fog behind. And high at the top was more of the same. Darkness. There was only darkness.

Deep-bellied yells erupted from around the deck. Searlus heard wails of petition to the Wavemaker, yells of order about an attack, and general panicked screams. Men went running around the deck, like the ship was going under. Searlus thought of Navas first, then Wayfinder Hemol. He made his way to the main deck, but before he could get further, the High Captain burst through the doors of his cabin, a sword and pistol hanging from his side, and stopped near Searlus. He looked up at the Lightholm and stared. Searlus saw the man's face go white.

"That's not possible," the High Captain said. "It's an

attack. An attack. We have to—" Before he could grasp the implications of the extinguished light before him, the familiar crack of cannon fire sounded across the bay. The cannonball whistled overhead and splashed into the water.

"Nimrad! Ready the boat!" he said.

More cannon blasts followed in rapid succession, the final one sounding as if it came from their own ship. Searlus looked toward the sound and saw a small single-masted sloop, a quarter of the size of the *Gildenglory* appearing from behind the sacred structure. Then another. And a third small ship. Flying high above their cannons, still smoking from use, was the unmistakable black flag with a singular white dot.

Zamarians.

Searlus snapped back to reality and the High Captain had vanished from his side. Searlus saw the man suspended over the edge of the ship in the small rowboat, being dropped into the bay. After a moment, he was gone for good. A flare of hot anger welled up in his bones. Before he could act on that heat, Kaius emerged from below deck. He clasped four or five swords in his hands, barely able to grip the handles.

"I think this is yours," he said, tossing a sword to Searlus. The silver blade soared through the air. Searlus stepped to the side. The heavy handle hit the wood plank floor with a thud. Kaius shook his head in disappointment before handing out more blades to every Horak he met. Searlus picked up the blade.

It was his family blade.

He wanted to ask Kaius how long he'd had the blade,

and how he came to possess it, but the floor of the ship shook under his feet. Searlus looked out over the rail, thinking they had struck the Lightholm. He could see the dark tower in the distance. Men screamed from the bow. They hadn't struck something.

Something had struck them.

From the flickering light of the few lamps hanging around the deck, a flood of quick movements danced around in the shadows. Then, all at once, a horde of Zamarians burst forth, screaming wild curses, long silver blades cutting the air. Without warning, a man with long, knotted black hair, deep, dark eyes, teeth missing, burst into the light. His sword, raised high in the air, swung down in a flash, and pierced through the closest Horak. Searlus could see the crimson tip sticking jagged out of the back of the fellow Horak. There was no scream. The man fell to his knees as the Zamarian pulled the blade loose. It all happened in a matter of seconds. The man fell to the ground, and the Zamarian hoard advanced in wild stampede.

Searlus was forced from his stupor when a younger, but equally decrepit-looking Zamarian charged across the deck toward him with the tip of his blade aimed at his heart.

"Where's our ship you dirty coxswain?"

At the last moment, Searlus swung his blade to parry the attack away. The Zamarian's forward momentum, intent to run the blade through Searlus, carried him forward until he crashed into his would-be victim. With the momentum from the parry, Searlus managed to extend his elbow at the last second so the man crashed into it, face first. The man still managed to tackle Searlus to the ground.

Warm drops of blood from the attacker's nose sprinkled Searlus' face as he recovered from crashing against the ground. He quickly got to his feet, careful not to drop his sword. The enemy was slow to recover, disoriented from the blow to the face. Searlus aimed his blade at the prostrate man and moved forward to run him through.

He didn't get the chance.

Before he knew it he was back on the ground. A scrawny figure had pushed and then tackled him onto the deck. A loud yell accompanied by hollow thuds echoed behind him. Searlus managed to turn and push the man away. The man did not try to attack further. Searlus readied his elbow to deal another blow in the close quarters, but before he struck he saw a familiar face on the ground beside him.

Kaius.

"What are you doing?" Searlus asked.

"Saved your tail, you fool," Kaius said, pointing behind Searlus. A large Zamarian with a sword in each hand had just lumbered past them in a reckless fury. His swords swung aimlessly as he thundered around the ship. Before Searlus could reply, a horn, like the call of a beast from Hadyl, roared from the top of the Lightholm.

The High Captain had sounded the alarm.

A moment later little fires flickered on in the distance in every direction. The men in the Isle of Hor were coming to protect the Lightholm. A burst of inspiration flared up inside of Searlus, lit by the fires on the shores.

He and Kaius pulled each other up to their feet. Kaius ran off into the skirmish without a second thought.

Searlus' eye caught movement on the shores of the Lightholm, like ants scurrying to their anthill. A small ship was anchored in the harbor.

Zamarians.

"I'll cover you, go!" Cora yelled behind him. She held her gun extended and the crack of gunpowder echoed through the bay as a Zamarian man fell off the side of the ship.

Without thinking, he ran to the side of the *Gildenglory* and dove headlong into the sea. He splashed into the warm water with his sword still firmly in his grip. He tied the blade to the rope around his waist and began the long swim to the Lightholm.

His mind was flooded with questions. Would he make it in time? Would he make it at all? Would the Zamarians burn the Lightholm? Had they killed everyone inside? Was there another beast waiting for him in the water?

Thoughts of not making it in time, or not making it at all, and of another Coiled Whale waiting for him wrecked him as he put one arm in front of the other and paddled to his destination. His arms, tired and malnourished, swept the water behind him, over and over, until finally he crashed into the dark rocks from which the Lightholm was built.

Searlus looked up and could see the dark Lightholm rising into the darker sky. As he crept up the wet rocks to the courtyard which held the imitation Harbor Stone, he noticed the fog had settled again over the entire isle. On the flat stone ground the sea dripped from him as he walked cautiously toward the Lightholm's open arches.

The silence was interrupted by hollow, wooden thuds. Searlus hid behind a pillar, opposite of the sound, and watched as men jumped from their rowboats, lanterns in one hand, swords in the other. Searlus remained hidden, for fear of being outnumbered in a fight. They were walking directly toward him as they prepared to seize the Lightholm. He held his breath as they passed, but a wave of relief washed over him when he heard one of the men speak.

"We hold the Lightholm, no matter what," a man said in a gruff, familiar voice. Searlus jumped out from behind the pillar and shouted.

"Dad!"

The Horak men jumped and raised their swords. Dovar did the same. Searlus dropped his sword and put his arms in the air. His father stepped forward, sword still poised, ready to attack, but with the lamp beside. He got close enough to see Searlus face.

"Searlus?" he asked. "The *Gildenglory* is back?"

"Why are the Zamarians attacking?" Searlus asked in return, but as the words left his mouth, he thought back to that deserted island, leaving the Zamarians stranded, and stealing their ship. A feeling like a stone weighed heavy in his stomach.

"We heard the horn, grabbed our swords. That's all we know."

"Are more of you coming?"

"No," his father said. "They're protecting the shores

to make sure the Zamarian wretches don't make it to land."

The sound of feet splashing, like horses galloping through a shallow creek, sounded behind them. The wet stampede turned into a steady drumming, accompanied by screams and yells. Dovar's men turned with their torches to reveal a new group of Zamarians attempting to invade the Lightholm.

The Horaks countered, with their own yells and wild screams, and charged the Zamarian horde and meeting them in the open courtyard. Searlus lifted his sword from the ground and did the same.

The Zamarians outnumbered the Horaks, but they fought as reckless individuals, whereas the Horaks, led by Searlus' father, fought in a tight formation, with disciplined, controlled strikes. Searlus lifted his sword to strike a nearby Zamarian, but the Zamarian raised his own jagged blade and blocked the strike. They went around in circles, both trying to get the upper hand, metal blades singing with every clash.

Despite the Zamarian's undisciplined fighting style, Searlus was unable to get the upper hand. Then, something in the distance caught Searlus' eye. Across the courtyard, a small orange ball of light bounced around across the front of the Lightholm before disappearing inside. The Horak men who arrived with his father were still fighting off the intruders, which only meant one thing.

The person who entered the Lightholm must have been a Zamarian.

Searlus swung his sword with a strong right slash,

which made the Zamarian block the blow by pulling his arm in tight. Searlus followed this attack with a swift, flat-footed kick. The Zamarian stumbled back, onto the jagged rocks that sloped into the sea, and was gone with a splash.

Searlus ran toward the Lightholm.

When he crossed the threshold into the Lightholm's ground floor, the sound of shouting and cannon fire were nearly muted. The stone walls of the Lightholm, meant to signify a barrier from the corruption of the outside world, provided insulation against the chaos waters surrounding it. Every sound inside the main floor was amplified, including the metallic clang of coins splashing onto the stone.

Searlus ducked behind a pillar yet again, slowly peering around it toward the sound. Across the room, the moonlight spilled in through the large archways and he could see a slender silhouetted figure shoving anything he could into a sack.

Searlus crept silently toward the Zamarian thief and felt self-righteous anger growing in him with every step. The tip of his sword led the way, ready to end the life of the person who dared desecrate the Lightholm. The figure continued its pillaging, blinded to the outside world by the unguarded gold coins. Searlus walked closer and closer until he was within range.

"Do you not fear the Wavemaker," Searlus asked in the deepest voice possible. He touched the tip of the sword to the back of the figure. "Turn around so I can run you through."

The man dropped the bag and lifted his hands in the

air. As he surrendered, he turned to face Searlus, less than an arms-length away. In the pale white light the smooth, beardless face of a Zamarian boy, not much older than twelve or thirteen, looked at Searlus with frightened eyes. Tears streaked down the boy's face.

Searlus stumbled backward at the revelation.

The boy seized the opportunity and in a split second, his face changed to a rage no child should know. He dropped his hands to his waist, grabbed his sword from its sheath, but before he could strike, he let out a high-pitched whelp.

The tip of Searlus' grandfather's sword was dripping crimson.

"Forgive me," the boy said, the words riding on his last breath. He fell limp on the blade.

Searlus pulled his sword free and dropped it to the ground, the metal and the flesh hitting the stone simultaneously. A moment later, from high up in the Lightholm, the horn bellowed.

Then, again.

And, a third time, signifying the Isles of Hor were safe.

Searlus sprinted toward the courtyard, toward his father, his mind as fogged as the harbor, hands shaking like the sea.

# 35

## INTO THE LIGHTHOLM

It was an impossibly hot morning in Tarsa, while inside a particular shop, where the clang of hammers crafting barrels used to ring daily, Searlus and Navas walked this way and that, packing up mallets and strips of metal. The stone shop did little to shield them from the heat, and acted more like an oven, slowly cooking everything inside.

"I'm keeping this," Searlus said, holding up a solid wood mallet, carved from a single log of oak. He slid it into a loop on the rope around his waist before returning to the stack of tools and placing them in a basket.

"Go for it," Navas said, packing up some of the scraps of metal.

"You taking anything? You'll get lonely up there. Need something to remind you of the good old days when you had a shop with your best friend."

Navas bent down and scooped up a handful of dirt from the ground. He sifted it in his hand.

"This seems like a good representation of my time here."

"Somebody is a bundle of joy this morning," Searlus said. Navas didn't reply but dropped the dirt and went back to packing up the shop. Searlus let the silence hang for a while before trying a different tact. "I'm going to miss this place, too."

"We were attacked three days ago," Navas said, with an edge to his voice. "Migdah was the first person they killed before snuffing out the flame. That's the job I'm going to do."

"Having second thoughts?"

"No," Navas said without hesitation. "If anything, it's confirmation for me. This will be the most important thing I do in my life. I won't let us get attacked again."

Searlus thought back to his encounter with the Zamarian boy on the ground floor of the Lightholm. He hadn't told anyone and did anything he could to keep his mind from thinking on it. He knew any Horak he asked would say he did the right thing, but that didn't mean it was good.

Before his mind could dwell any longer, a soft knock sounded at the door. Searlus' mother stepped in.

"Mom?" Searlus asked.

"Sorry," she said. Her eyes were puffy and red.

"No, no, come in, Elitza," Navas said. "I need to run to the market and need someone to talk to this yapping fox." Elitza laughed and stepped in, leaving the door open. Navas wiped his hands on his cloak before making his way to the door. "Be right back." Then he closed the door behind him.

"You alright, Mom?"

"Yeah. Me? Yeah, I'm okay. It's your dad."

"Are you hurt?" Searlus asked, standing up straight.

"No, no, nothing like that," she said. "He just won't shut up. If I hear another story about all the Zamarians he killed I'm going to have him add me to his list."

"He might have enjoyed it a little too much," Searlus said.

"Highlight of his life. No question," she said. She walked over to a simple wooden chair and sat down. "That's not why I'm here, though." Searlus found a chair across from her and sat down.

"Okay," he said, leaving the space for her to continue.

"It's Devora."

"Where is she?"

"I don't know," his mom said, her voice cracking. "She was..." her voice trailed off. Searlus didn't say anything. "She was living down by the Saluman temple. Doing..." her voice trailed off again, silence followed by sobs.

"I know, Mom," Searlus said.

"My daughter is a whore," she said, tears flowing freely.

"She's not doing that anymore. I talked to her before I left."

"She hasn't been around since then. Following that magician from Kedess around. There's a whole group of them. The Saluman government is starting to take notice."

"I'll find her," Searlus said. "I'll bring her home."

"People are talking, Searlus. Saying that magician is

going to lead some kind of rebellion. There was a small riot in Golaun when you were gone. Horaks beaten and imprisoned. Devora's going to get herself killed," his mom said, bursting into tears again.

Before Searlus could reply, there was a loud knock at the door. Elitza tried to compose herself. Searlus went to the door and pulled it open. Standing outside was a fellow Horak in full captain attire, complete with the golden sun pin on his shoulder.

"Searlus of Ramooth?" the man asked.

"Yes sir."

"My name is Maliel of Shakum, a Captain in the Holy Fleethood. I report directly to the High Captain, and he has requested your presence at the Lightholm."

"Oh, okay," Searlus said, looking back to his mom. "When?"

"You are to come with me."

"Is there trouble?"

"Yes," Maliel said. "The High Captain wants to appoint a new task force to eliminate this 'magician of Kedess' problem, and he needs a new captain to lead it."

Searlus looked back to his mother, and in her sad eyes and dark hair, he could see his sister, hurting and tricked by this new cult. He turned back to the man and said.

"Let me get my cloak."

~

**SEARLUS WILL RETURN.**

~

# KEEP THE STORY GOING
## DISCUSSION QUESTIONS
### (SPOILERS AHEAD!)

1. How are Searlus and Navas attitudes toward the Salumans similar? How are they different?

2. Does Searlus seem to share more of his personality with his mother or father? Why?

3. If Searlus was the leader of the Horaks, if he was the High Captain, how do you think he would confront the Saluman Empire?

4. Do you think Searlus is going to fulfill his part of the oath? If yes, how so? If no, why not?

5. What did Searlus do right as "acting captain" of the Oathslaker? What could he have done better?

6. The High Captain is supposed to be the best of the Horaks, how does the High Captain do this well? Where does he fall short?

7. During the Zamarian attack, Searlus finally got to put his violent solution into practice. How do you think he's feeling after killing the Zamarian?

8. What do you think will be the biggest obstacle Searlus will face when investigating the Magician?

# About the Author

F.C. Shultz is an author and poet whose work has been published in Ekstasis Magazine, Every Day Fiction, and the *Of Gods and Globes* anthologies. He's published a handful of middle grade and young adult novels.

He's trying to cultivate a deep appreciation for the simple pleasures, which means writing a lot of poems about birds (and novels about dragons). He lives in the Midwest with his wife and two kids.

You can find stories and other author resources at fcshultz.com.

# ABOUT THE PUBLISHER

Daath Stone Books exists to publish fantastical kidlit for fantastic kids. We don't write down for children. In fact, we do the opposite. We believe our best work should be for children.

Find more fantastical books at **daathstonebooks.com.**

 facebook.com/daathstonebooks

www.ingramcontent.com/pod-product-compliance
Lightning Source LLC
Chambersburg PA
CBHW022200170626
46807CB00005B/2284